"You've Been Sent Out Here To Keep Me Under Surveillance,"

Beth said.

Brian said nothing. How could he deny what was so obviously true?

"Well?" she prodded him.

"How can I explain to you when you're in this state?"

That meant he didn't have any explanation. "All right," she informed him in a voice as frosty as a glacier. "It's a public trail. I can't stop you from walking it. But not with me. If you have to do your spying, you can do it from a distance. And if you don't keep behind me and out of my way, I'll report you for harassment at the first opportunity."

Not waiting for his reaction, Beth swung off ahead of him with the stride of a marathon walker.

"Hey, Yank," he shouted as he watched her go. "You start off with that kind of gait, you'll drop before you're ever out of Georgia."

Dear Reader:

Welcome to Silhouette Desire—sensual, compelling, believable love stories written by and for today's woman. When you open the pages of a Silhouette Desire, you open yourself up to a whole new world—a world of promising passion and endless love.

Each and every Silhouette Desire is a wonderful love story that is both sensuous *and* emotional. You're with the hero and heroine each and every step of the way—from their first meeting, to their first kiss . . . to their happy ending. You'll experience all the deep joys—and occasional tribulations—of falling in love.

In future months, look for Silhouette Desire novels from some of your favorite authors, such as Annette Broadrick, Dixie Browning, Kathleen Korbel and Lass Small, just to name a few.

So go wild with Desire. You'll be glad you did!

Lucia Macro
Senior Editor

JEAN
BARRETT
HOT ON HER TRAIL

SILHOUETTE *Desire*

Published by Silhouette Books New York

America's Publisher of Contemporary Romance

SILHOUETTE BOOKS
300 East 42nd St., New York, N.Y. 10017

ISBN: 0-373-05574-9

First Silhouette Books printing June 1990

JEAN BARRETT

always dreamed of being a successful writer. After much rejection and despair, Jean has attained that dream! Of course, the lucky part is that she has a supportive, patient, loving spouse who was there every step of the way.

A former teacher who traded the classroom for a typewriter, Jean loves the great outdoors, antiques and cross-country skiing. But she thinks that nothing is more pleasurable than reading.

For my sister, Nancy,
with love

One

Here I am, sweetheart, ready and willing to go all the way with you.''

The tall figure who stood in the open doorway of Beth Holland's rural Georgia motel room was a complete stranger. He didn't seem to realize that, however. He went on grinning at her in a much too friendly fashion.

Beth stared at him in silent astonishment. His arms were flung out in an attitude that seemed to be inviting an intimate embrace. And just what had he meant by that eager announcement with which she had been instantly greeted when she opened the door to his brash knock? She was afraid to guess.

''Ready and willing? Look, I think you've got the wrong room.'' And probably the wrong idea, she thought, beginning to suspect the worst. Maybe this guy had arranged in advance for some fun and games at the local motel and was wrongly assuming she was the object of his intentions.

His gaze went confidently to the number on her door. "Don't think so. Beth Holland, number 18. That's what the girl at the desk told me, anyway, when I stopped at the office to look for you. That's right, isn't it?"

She didn't answer him. She was much too surprised to form an immediate response, though slightly relieved to see that the powerful arms that looked as though they'd been ready to get familiar with her had been lowered to his sides. How on earth had he gotten her name?

Wary now, Beth eyed him with mounting distrust. She wasn't encouraged by what she saw. Frankly, he was a mess. His Western boots had seen better days and were caked with mud; the faded jeans above them were filthy and torn; the terrible Hawaiian shirt—the wildest she'd ever seen—was stained and rumpled. His baseball cap was tilted over a face bleary-eyed and badly needing a shave. That cap was decorated with, of all things, bottle caps. How could a person come up with such a mismatched outfit? She presumed the equally dirty and battered pickup truck parked behind him was his. The man had all the appearance of a disreputable transient. Was there a risk factor here?

"What?" he asked innocently, aware now of her suspicious stare. When she continued to stare, his eyes turned up to the visor of the baseball cap and then traveled down his long and solid length to the muddy tips of his boots. "Right, I see what you mean. Well, it's like this...." He began to explain to her cheerfully in a deep voice with a slight Georgia drawl that carried absolutely no trace of self-consciousness. "There was this all-night country music jamboree far downstate, which is where I've just come from. Everybody dresses casually for jamborees."

An understatement, Beth thought, standing impatiently at the door as she wondered how she was going to get rid of him. She didn't need this, not today of all days.

"I hadn't had any sleep when I got in from the jamboree, see, and then the call came. I didn't even take time to change. I just threw all my gear into the truck and took off. Been driving just about all day to get here, and worst luck, I ran into a real gully-washer. Had to wrestle the truck out of a muddy ditch, which is why I look so awful. End of explanation."

Not by half, Beth thought, but she wasn't going to urge him for more details. All she wanted was to close the door on him, although that might take some doing. One of the big Western boots was half over the threshold.

He met her silence with a clearing of the throat. "So, why don't I find a room back in town? Couldn't get anything here close to you. The motel is full up because of the annual Goober Festival. Peanut country, you know. I'll check in somewhere, get cleaned up, head back here, and then we can get down to business."

There was that lewd-sounding, possibly even illegal suggestion again. He was definitely beginning to worry her. She tried for a polite firmness. "I think we have a tiny mistake here. Obviously, you think you're expected, but I don't know you from Adam, and I can't imagine how you got my name. I'm not sure at this point I even want to know because, to tell you the truth, I don't think I care for what you might be proposing, but if you'll just quietly go away, I promise I'll forget— What call?"

"The one from Hobart in Atlanta. Don't tell me they neglected to let you know I was coming?"

Beth could feel her determined jaw sagging. "Hobart phoned you? Hobart Development Company phoned you and brought you here? *That* Hobart?"

"I think it's the only one, sweetheart. At least in Atlanta."

"I've been out all day shopping for last-minute necessities and making arrangements to garage my car, so if they did try to reach me— Hobart called you about me?" Beth couldn't seem to grasp this small revelation. "But why? What's this all about?"

"That." He sliced a strong, deeply tanned hand in the direction of the backpacking gear that was strewn around the room behind her. "According to Atlanta, the essentials are: Beth Holland is scheduled bright and early tomorrow morning to begin hiking the Appalachian Trail. Personally, I consider the circumstances of this whole deal slightly peculiar, but who am I to say? Hobart seems to have got itself connected with this haul. Though if you want my opinion, I don't think they took your little verbal arrangement with them too seriously. Not, anyway, until the next day when that item appeared in the Atlanta paper about what you were undertaking and why. Smart move on your part, I'd say, to go public with it. They have to take you for real now, don't they, or else look bad? That's when they suddenly started to get worried about your being out there on the trail all on your own. If something should happen to you and the company's name is involved, they wind up looking responsible. Not good for the image, Beth.

"Which is where Brian McArdle comes in. That's me. Since I have some experience with backpacking, will I accompany Ms. Holland? Even if it is the long one, Georgia to Maine? Sure, why not? Figuring, you know, it ought to be an interesting challenge. Anyway, I pulled off the last construction project, which is the actual reason I was downstate since I work out in the field a lot for the company. I hightailed it north for this here town that's the jumping-off place for the A.T., where I'm told I can expect to find Ms. Holland at the Rest Easy Motel. So that's why

I'm here, and basically that's all I know. You can fill me in on the details yourself. That is, if you care to.''

Beth's initial reaction was amazement that he had been able to deliver his lengthy explanation without pausing for breath. He was now lounging with perfect ease against her doorframe, arms folded over the broad chest of the awful Hawaiian shirt.

Her next move was a big mistake. "Then *that's* what you meant by going all the way with me." The relieved words were out of her mouth before she could stop them.

The bleary but alert eyes under the baseball cap brightened with mischief. "Why, Beth, you have a naughty mind.''

Beth knew she was turning a hot pink, but she couldn't help it. "Well, what do you expect when you show up at my door looking like—when your arms were—when the first words out of your mouth . . . Oh, you know what I mean.''

He was grinning that impudent grin again. "I think I do, sweetheart.''

Beth's jaw was still drooping from mild shock. She resolutely tightened it, stiffening her five-foot-one-and-three-quarter-inch frame in the process. This situation had to be handled, but she wasn't quite sure how. She went for a pleasant but brisk tone of voice. "All right, Brian Mc-whatever, we have a problem here that needs settling, but before we discuss it, will you please do me the small favor of not calling me 'sweetheart' anymore? Not, you understand, that I want to be a drag about it, but I just sort of mind a bit when—''

"McArdle.''

"Pardon?''

"The name is McArdle, remember? Brian McArdle.''

"Fine. So, like I say—''

"You're a Yankee.''

"Huh?"

"That explains it, Beth. Yankees don't understand when we Southerners go around calling everybody 'sweetheart' or 'honey.' They think we're being too personal. We're not. We're just being warm and friendly. Harmless, see."

The man was a nut case! A genuine, six-foot, muscle-bound nut case! How was she going to make him see reason? She had to try. "Could we please just get this mess sorted out?"

"What mess? I thought it was all simple and straightforward. I walk with you from Georgia to Maine, right?"

"Wrong. What you do is turn around and drive back to Atlanta, where you tell the Hobart people that their company has no responsibility whatever for my welfare on the trail. Hobart Development is not sponsoring the hike. In fact, they very much want this hike not to succeed at all. Therefore, it makes no sense for me to accept the services of their bodyguard."

"Image, Beth, remember?"

"Hobart doesn't need to worry about my safety. I'm a professional naturalist. I know what I'm doing."

"All on your own out there? That doesn't sound smart to me," he pointed out, still lounging against the doorframe. "Not with the wildlife that could be hanging around some of those trail shelters. The two-legged variety, that is."

"I can take care of myself. I won't be the first to hike the trail alone. And women have done it as well, if that's what you're thinking. I told you I'm experienced."

"With the long-haul stuff, Beth?"

"Not that kind of distance, no," she admitted. "But the nature of my work demands that I keep in top physical shape at all times."

"Yeah," he conceded, the drawl turning low and husky. "I can see that all right."

Another mistake. Bloodshot or not, his eyes were an incredible, disturbing blue-green. At the moment those disarming blue-greens where checking out the less athletic qualities of her figure with an interest that for some incomprehensible reason had rapid flutters chasing through the bottom of her stomach.

Oh, Lord, no, she didn't want this sort of complication. She had enough to contend with here as it was. *Come on, Beth, don't stand here like a moron. Deal with it.*

"The point being," she said with an assurance she was far from actually feeling, "I just don't need your protection. I appreciate Hobart's last-minute concern, and I'm sorry you were persuaded to drop everything and rush up here like this. But I'm asking you to go back to Atlanta and forget all about it."

"Oh, I don't think I could do that, Beth." He shook his head solemnly. "The company wouldn't like it, you see."

She's small, Brian thought as he went on boldly measuring her. Probably wouldn't reach the height of my chin if she stood on tiptoe. But it didn't matter. He could see she was all woman, although that baggy top and the comfortably loose slacks she wore didn't help. He wondered what lay under them. Something lush and responsive to the right touch, he'd bet.

Damn, what had he walked into? He hadn't reckoned on this when he'd agreed to come up here. "Nothing complicated," he had been promised. And here he was already having to rethink his strategy and consider possibilities he had no business entertaining.

Beth's frustration was beginning to peak. "This is weird. People don't do things like this. They don't overnight drop their lives to go off for weeks on end into the wilderness with a total stranger. Not responsible people."

But she had to face it, it wasn't his irresponsibility that was worrying her. It was his wide, sensual mouth behind the two days' growth of whiskers. She didn't think she trusted that mouth. No, she *knew* she didn't.

"I'm responsible," he insisted. "It's why the company picked me."

He simply wasn't going to walk away. It wasn't going to be that easy. How could a reputable firm like Hobart Development send out a character like this to represent them? All-night jamborees and baseball caps with bottle caps! She'd have to check on his claim, not just take his word for it. She'd have to phone Atlanta. Maybe Hobart hadn't sent him. For all she knew, he could be an escapee from some asylum. "Just what sort of work do you do for the company?" she asked him suspiciously.

"Mmm, kind of a job troubleshooter, I guess you'd say."

Whatever that meant. It sounded far too general. "Then how can Hobart spare you for a whole season? That's what it'll take to walk from Georgia to Maine."

"I'm a hell of a troubleshooter by long distance, Beth, and I think there are phones along the trail."

This was maddening. He was calmly countering her every objection, and the more agitated she became, the more relaxed he grew leaning there in her doorway. She wasn't going to let him do this to her. "Mr. McArdle—Brian—you can't go with me, and that is that."

"Why? The reasons you've already given me don't sound very solid, and the fact that you're obviously the independent, stubborn type is something I kind of admire but it could get you in hot water out on that trail."

But Beth knew why. Whatever else lurked under all that hard-hat grime and goofiness, good or bad, there was the indisputable, and probably lethal, combination of his blue-green eyes and melting Dixie drawl. Admittedly, this might make for an interesting development, maybe even of the raw animal variety, but she didn't think she cared to risk it. Not when she had this all-important hike to concentrate on. She didn't need anything potentially sizzling to distract her!

Beth decided that a simple brusqueness might be a lot safer than an honest, emotional spilling of her guts. "Listen," she pleaded, "let's just be reasonable here and—"

"Good idea." He straightened up in the doorway. "I'll go find that room, get myself cleaned up. You'll like me a whole lot better cleaned up. Maybe I'll even catch a quick catnap, and that will give you a chance to phone Hobart, who will convince you I'm the genuine article. Just in case you have any doubts." So he reads minds, too. "Then you and I can meet in the coffee shop down at the end there in—" he consulted his watch "—say about two hours? Neutral ground, Beth, to discuss our plans for tomorrow. Now that's reasonable, isn't it?"

Lifting his hand in a careless salute, he turned away and started for his truck.

Beth called after him in a panic, "Wait! You can't just walk off! We haven't settled—"

"Two hours, Beth."

The pickup truck roared out of the parking lot, leaving Beth standing in the motel doorway feeling as though she had just been steamrollered by some mountainous piece of construction equipment.

Within seconds, Beth was on the phone to Atlanta, praying she could sort out this awkward predicament.

"Hobart Development Company." The receptionist-secretary's voice was bright and affable.

"This is Beth Holland calling. Could I speak to Mr. Hobart, please?" The was a long pause. Beth could feel the woman's sudden caution. "It's very important," she added.

"Yes. I'll see if he's available, Ms. Holland. It may take a couple of minutes. I believe he's in the planning department right now with a client."

"I'll hold."

Why did she have the impression that the woman was stalling? It was understandable, of course, that the Hobart people might be regarding her with less than warmth when she was challenging their rights to a valuable strip of property, but this had been more than mere coolness. It had been—what? A kind of uneasiness, as though Beth might find out something she wasn't supposed to? No, that was silly.

While waiting for Charles Hobart to come to the phone, Beth remembered her first contact with the head of Hobart Development Company. Her reception then had been entirely cordial and open. Even when she faced Charles Hobart in his office and he learned from her that she was there to appeal to him on behalf of the Appalachian Trail, he had remained pleasant.

A slight man whose thinning hair and rather dry, formal manner made him seem much older than his thirty-two years, he had smiled at her across his desk, answering her without reservation. "Yes, the Maine property. We acquired it just this year, and as you've pointed out, it's a beautiful section of wooded land lying between two unspoiled lakes. We have great plans for it—a private luxury resort with condos, golf course and tennis, the works. In fact, it's our most ambitious project to date," he added proudly. "And the first time we're to go interstate. But you say you're already informed about this, Ms. Holland. How is that?"

"As I mentioned, I represent the Green Guards, which is a country-wide environmental society that actively supports the Appalachian Trail Conference. The society keeps aware of everything that deals with wilderness preservation. Because there is this threat to a section of the Appalachian Trail—well, since I was to be in Atlanta anyway for a few days visiting a friend and since I am qualified to discuss the situation, the Green Guards asked me to call on you."

"Qualified how, Ms. Holland?"

"For one thing, I'm a professional naturalist employed by the Green Guards at one of their Mississippi River sanctuaries in my home state of Wisconsin, though I'm currently on a leave of absence for six months." No point in explaining why. It wouldn't matter to him. "And for another," she went on, "I'm familiar with that particular property in Maine."

"The friend you're visiting? Also connected with the Green Guards?"

"No, she's an Atlanta housewife and a publicist who works out of her home. We've been close ever since we were kids. You see, the Hobart land in Maine is where Annie and I first met. My uncle once owned and operated the property as a summer camp. It was called Camp Sweetwater after the bigger of the two lakes, and Annie and I were sent there every August by our folks. That's where we both learned to have a special respect and affection for the wilderness."

Beth tried to give him just enough information to permit him to appreciate her position. But with only a few cold facts, how could she make him understand how important that land was in relation to the trail. Her Uncle Ray had taught her and scores of other young people to value the environment. Even after they had outgrown their summer camp years, she and Annie had returned in their teens to act as counselors. These precious experiences had led Beth to pursue a career as a naturalist. What she was telling him seemed so inadequate, but she didn't think Charles Hobart was the kind of man who would relate to emotional arguments.

"That makes it a little clearer," he said when she finished. "I gather you see yourself, then, as having—ah, a kind of personal stake in all this?"

She leaned toward him, unable to contain her deep earnestness. "Not in any legal sense, of course. I know that land was sold long ago, after my uncle's death, but he and the owner after him always permitted the Appalachian Trail a right-of-way between the two lakes."

"And now our development is to lie smack across that right-of-way." Beth could see that he thought she was being naive and sentimental. "You do realize this right-of-way was never anything more than a verbal arrangement, not legally binding. But Hobart isn't being heartless in the matter. We're donating a relocation for the trail at the far end of the smaller of the two lakes. This is acceptable to the National Park Service, which as you must know is a protector of the A.T."

"Acceptable, maybe, but far from desirable. There are acres of swampy land out there, just as there are at the end of the other lake. The cost to cut and raise a new section of trail through there would be staggering, and it could be a long time before the funds were available. We both know that government agencies are long on promises and short on cash."

His smile deepened, taking on a patronizing quality she didn't care for. "Ms. Holland, what do you want me to do? Offer to let the trail continue to run right through our development?"

Yes, that was exactly what both Beth and the Green Guards wanted. "Would it interfere so much with your project, Mr. Hobart? A narrow footpath taking up a minimum of space when you have all the rest of that acreage in there to build on?''

''It wouldn't be in the best interests of our project, Ms. Holland. Luxury resorts require privacy.'' The smile never left his face, but it was decidedly condescending now. ''Aren't you exaggerating the value of a trail through there? What does it really matter if the A.T. is interrupted at that point? Frankly, I don't see that a two-thousand-mile un-broken wilderness footpath is of benefit to anyone but— well, forgive me for putting it this way—a handful of nature freaks who have the fanciful notion that one day someone might want to walk that whole distance in one trip.''

He doesn't know, was Beth's first amazed thought. Charles Hobart actually did not know. He had slipped up on his homework with this one, failing to realize that every spring dozens of hikers started out from Georgia with the intention of trekking the A.T. all the way to its northern terminus in Maine. A few of those backpackers even made it. But whether they did or did not, it was essential to pre-serve every inch of the Appalachian Trail against any threatening invasions of concrete and asphalt. Beth be-lieved this without question. Maybe there was a way to let Hobart Development know just how much she did care.

That was when the inspiration hit her. She had always dreamed of one day walking the trail anyway. Why not now, and for a worthy motive? The Green Guards had asked her to do whatever she could to persuade Hobart to keep that portion of the trail intact, so she felt they would support and fund her plan. The circumstances were certainly in her favor. The season was right, and she still had more than four months left of her six-month leave of absence. She had thought those months would be necessary when her step-father died. She had returned to her childhood home in a Milwaukee suburb to help her mother settle her affairs and

sell the house. But considering how dependent she had always been on her husband, Beth's mother was already
managing beautifully.

She hesitated. Would she be taking advantage of Charles
Hobart's ignorance if she seized this opportunity? She gazed
at him across his too-neat desk, undecided. The superior
little smile was still on his thin mouth, and it made her mad.
Beth read that smile like a direct challenge, and she rose to
it instantly.

"Mr. Hobart," she said quietly, "I have a proposition for
you."

She explained her offer, and if nothing else, she did
achieve the satisfaction of wiping that offensive smile from
his face. For a moment, he looked positively startled. "Are
you serious, Ms. Holland? You are proposing to demon-
strate the value of a continuous trail by hiking it yourself
from Georgia to Maine in one trip?"

"That's right. And like I say, if I make it all the way with
no more than one-night stopovers and leaving the trail only
to buy essentials in adjacent towns, then Hobart Development guarantees a protected wilderness corridor through its
project. Think of the potential publicity, Mr. Hobart. Your
company could get a lot of favorable attention for just allowing me to try this. I'm sure the Green Guards would want
to hire the services of my friend to promote the hike, and
Annie is a very good publicist." She didn't miss the gleam
in his eye at the mention of publicity, and she knew she had
zeroed in on his weakness. "Will you consider it?" she
pressed.

He regarded her in silence for a full minute, and when the
smirky smile crept back to his lips, Beth knew exactly what
he was thinking. He was amused by her "little crusade," by
the unlikelihood of any female so small and seeming so fragile hiking as far as the Carolinas, never mind an uninter-

rupted two thousand miles to Maine. He didn't know how tough and resilient she could be.

Maybe in the end it was just his easy way of getting rid of her, not believing she actually meant it, or maybe it was a kind of pompous overconfidence when he promised rashly, "Ms. Holland, if you can actually walk two thousand miles from Georgia to Maine in one trip, then I think you can count on Hobart giving you your trail through the development."

That had been two days ago. Now when Charles Hobart finally came on the line he sounded as reluctant to hear from her as his secretary. Clearly, he was regretting his reckless promise, probably wishing there were some way he could withdraw it. He couldn't, without risking his company's credibility during a sensitive stage of expansion. Annie had seen to that. Through her media connections, she had secured a human interest story in one of the Atlanta papers the day after Beth's meeting with Charles Hobart. Beth Holland's arrangement with Hobart Development was now public knowledge.

Charles's voice was flat and humorless as he spoke to her. "Ms. Holland? My office has been trying all day to reach you."

Strange, she thought. They'd wanted to contact her, and now that they had, there was this restraint.

He went on. "There is something we need to let you know."

"Your representative—if that's the word for him—is here. He showed up on my doorstep a few minutes ago. That is what you wanted to let me know, isn't it?"

There was an awkward pause before his brief, "Yes."

"Then that's why I've called. Mr. Hobart, I appreciate your concern for my well-being, but I assure you I don't need any protector out on the trail." Beth went on with all the same arguments she had offered Brian McArdle, ending with an uncomfortable, "Besides, your man is—um—well, rather unusual, isn't he?" And that's putting it mildly, she thought.

"Brian McArdle is perfectly reliable, Ms. Holland, and he is the one condition I make to our agreement."

"But—"

"I'm sorry," he insisted bluntly, "but either McArdle goes with you to assure us of your safety, or our deal is off."

"I see. Well, if you put it like that—"

"I assume we'll be hearing from time to time what progress you're making out there. Good luck, Ms. Holland."

And that was it. He hung up without another word.

Damn! What was going on? she asked herself. The whole mood on Hobart's end had been abrupt, even evasive.

Beth went on sitting cross-legged on the floor of her motel room, the phone still in her lap, as she tried to determine whether she had something legitimate to worry about. There might, she realized, be a way of finding out what was happening at Hobart. If, in fact, something *was* happening that she ought to know about. Annie. She needed to bounce all these developments off her friend anyway.

Beth picked up the phone and placed a second call to Atlanta.

"'lo," answered a small voice.

"Andrew, is that you?"

"Uh-huh."

"This is Beth calling. Can I talk to your mother, hon?"

"Okay." The phone was thumped down on Annie's desk in her office corner of the family room, and Beth heard six-year-old Andrew shouting, "*Mo-om*, it's for you, and Becky's screwing up the TV again!"

Beth waited, listening with a smile to the familiar background noise of the two children squabbling, the TV blasting, the dog yipping excitedly and Annie yelling something in the distance. There was never not a crisis in her friend's happy-go-lucky household.

The angular Annie, all sass and chopped-off hair, finally snatched up the receiver with a breathless, "Beth? Where are you calling from? Becky, turn down the TV! *Now!*"

"From the motel. Listen, something has come up." Beth proceeded to give her the particulars.

Annie, who was always quick to spot the significance of any situation, was ready to agree with her. "Mmm, you're right. Sounds fishy to me."

"I hope not. I hope it's just what it appears to be, a concern for my safety, but with all your connections there in Atlanta, I thought, well, maybe you could have heard something."

"Not yet, but I'll ask around. People talk, especially when they're not supposed to. Could be I can come up with an explanation to this little mystery. And Dick hears stuff out there in the business community, too. See, I told you this arrangement with Hobart was too easy. I don't trust 'em."

Beth was suddenly doubtful. "Annie, maybe you shouldn't be playing detective for me. I'm sure the Hobart outfit must be an honest one, or they wouldn't have agreed to the hike in the first place, and I wouldn't want—"

Annie cut her off with a loud snort. "Listen, there's something important at stake here, and if Hobart is starting to play dirty, don't you think we ought to know about it?"

"That's only *if.*"

"It's enough for me. Besides, there's no way I'm going to be left out of this campaign. If I can't be out there tramping beside you, then at least I intend doing my part here in Atlanta. Heck, it's only a matter of listening. But, look, I'm going to keep up with all the PR angle, too. Properly handled, I think I can get some really decent media attention sympathetic to your cause. Your Green Guard bosses seemed to like what I've lined up when I talked to them.''

Beth had the uneasy feeling that her friend was hugely enjoying the whole show. "That's fine, Annie. Oh, I got a response from the Appalachian Trail Conference people this afternoon, and they're sanctioning the hike, too. Look, I'd better let you go now."

"Oh, no, you don't! Not before I hear all about this guy—this Brian McArdle character they're sending you. You hardly said boo about *him*. I can smell you holding back. What's he like? Exactly what does he do for Hobart?''

Beth hesitated, then decided that Annie would pry it out of her, anyway. "He claims he's a kind of troubleshooter, whatever that means. Hard to say with all the soil and the funny uniform, but judging from the size of him, he looks more like one of their construction workers. *Heavy* construction.''

"Ho-ho!"

"What's that supposed to mean?''

"It means," Annie said, and Beth could imagine her grin, "that I get the picture. Very big all over and very, *very* male.''

"Annie—''

"You gonna let him tag along?''

"I don't seem to have any choice in the matter.''

"I am not happy about this, Beth.''

"Ann—''

"Remember your record when it comes to mixing causes with men. Especially the heavy construction types. Becky, stop chewing on the dog's leg. Do you want to give him rabies?''

Beth welcomed the interruption. "I thought it was Tina who was teething."

"She is. This is just Becky's cute way of telling me she's hungry and it's time I started dinner. All right, I'm hanging up, but not before I give you your orders. Remember, once you're out there, I can't call you. You have to check in with me. Regularly."

"Got it."

"And—most important of all—watch yourself with Mr. Heavy Construction. Don't forget: he's on the other side. Oh, you can believe," she cooed, "I am *especially* going to find out all about him."

This was getting heavy, Beth decided with a silent groan as she said a hasty goodbye to Annie and replaced the phone on the bedside table. She had yet to take her first step on the A.T., and already things were going on that were uncomfortable.

What was she going to do about Brian McArdle? What else could she do but accept him? Maybe Hobart was right. Maybe she didn't have any business tackling this thing on her own. Two thousand miles and a lot of it brutal terrain. It had defeated plenty of others. Maybe, alone, she didn't stand a chance of conquering the trail either. Except, why did they want to help her when they stood to lose if she made it all the way to Maine? It didn't make sense.

You're being too suspicious, Beth. It's like Brian said: anything should happen to you out there, and it reflects against the company. That's all.

She wished that were all of it. It wasn't. She was still confronted by the daunting prospect of being out on that trail for weeks on end with a man who, only minutes after she'd met him, was driving her crazy.

Forget him, Beth. Just put him out of your mind until you have to face him in the coffee shop. Time enough then to deal with this provocative situation.

Good, because there was another job demanding her attention, one she had been undertaking when Brian interrupted—the sorting and packing of the equipment that was to accompany her. It was time she resumed her work.

With a distance like this ahead of her, it was imperative that she bear the lightest possible load. That meant that she must ruthlessly weed out all but the absolute essentials from the gear she had either bought today or borrowed from Annie's family. Quite a collection of equipment was spread around the motel room floor: all-weather poncho, mummy-style sleeping bag, assorted freeze-dried food, sandwich-size butane stove, various utensils and some personal effects, including the bare necessities where clothing was concerned. The combined weight of all these things, she knew, was not as awesome as it appeared. They were made of feather-light materials, but every ounce still mattered. That was why she had already decided to leave Annie's two-person nylon tent behind. Though the Appalachian Trail shelters were sometimes without vacancies during this time of the year, if she had to, she could sleep in the open. She had managed it before.

It took quite a while to discard the nonvital items and then to load and reload the two-compartment backpack until she was satisfied with both weight and distribution. Everything she'd eliminated would be packed in her two suitcases, which the motel had kindly agreed to store until Annie was able to drive up from Atlanta to collect them.

From long practice, her hands performed the work almost automatically. It was a good thing, too, because her brain was refusing to obey her earlier promise to herself. She couldn't seem to stop herself from thinking about the man who was scheduled to go with her tomorrow. Lord, had he made that much of an impression on her after an encounter of a few brief minutes? He had. And a strong one. Bottle caps and Hawaiian orchids aside, Brian McArdle, it seemed, was one of those men who possesses a bigger-than-life presence, who doesn't just occupy his space but dominates it, charging it with his energy and humor.

Maddening. Stop dwelling on him, dummy. Get down to business here. You almost forgot the A.T. maps and guide. You go on like this, and you'll never see Maine.

A glance at her watch when she was finally finished assured her there was still time for a quick shower and change before she had to meet Brian in the coffee shop.

When she got out of the shower Beth hurried. She didn't want to be late and risk having Hobart's knight-errant banging at her door again. The thick braid hanging down her back was in disorder, untidy tendrils escaping from all sides. There was no time to repair it. Easier to free her hair and wear it loose. Unbinding the braid, she rapidly brushed the mane of luxuriant chestnut waves that fell softly to below her shoulders. She didn't bother with makeup. She seldom did, except for lipstick and maybe a touch of shadow to enhance a pair of spirited brown eyes flecked with warm amber. Her face was attractive enough. A small depression at the end of her nose lent it a winsome quality.

Beth was reaching for fresh jeans and a clean top when her eye was caught by the temptation hanging on the bathroom door—a cotton shirtwaist in a green summery print, one of the few dresses she had brought with her to Georgia. She started mechanically to reach for the dress and then pulled back. Wait a minute. Just what image was she after here? And why?

What do you think you're doing, Beth?

Pleasing myself, that's what. Nobody but myself. Right?

Right.

It was probably the last dress she would see on herself for months, coffee shop setting or not. So what the heck, why not?

Shirtwaist in place and belted, she slipped on a pair of low-heeled sandals and hastily exited from her room.

A spring twilight had settled on the motel grounds, the air balmy and scented with blossom, the waxen luster of a flowering magnolia looking luminously white in the fading light.

Beth moved along the walkway toward the glare of the coffee shop, remembering that Brian had said he was going to clean up. She couldn't help it. She had to wonder what she was going to find under the dirt and the stubble. Maybe nothing that meant anything. That would be a relief, wouldn't it?

The place was noisy and crowded with Goober Festival-goers. She stood just inside the entrance, scanning the tables. He didn't seem to be there. She refused to admit the depth of her sudden disappointment.

She let her gaze wander again, checking the room to be sure. Her eyes slid over a rangy figure standing guard over a recently vacated booth at the rear, then zoomed back in shocked recognition.

Two

Wow!

A mundane expression, Beth realized, but it did suitably convey the sledgehammer impact of discovering precisely what had been hiding under the baseball cap, the Hawaiian shirt, the dirt and whiskers, the—well, all the rest.

Another Brian McArdle had emerged, this one clad in crisp tan slacks and a spotless white knit shirt. The outfit was plain and presentable. On any other man it would have been respectably dull. On him it managed to reinforce blatantly what her earlier encounter with him had indicated—a forceful, even blazing virility.

Maybe she was overreacting. On the other hand, maybe her emotional state was warning her to turn around and make a run for it. Too late. He had looked up and found her. The expressive blue-green eyes, noticing she had undergone a transformation of her own, were registering a surprise and pleasure equal to Beth's.

He was waiting for her, his slow grin inviting her to join him. She had no choice but to bring herself contact-close to that potent six-footer with his blade of a nose and the curly mop of sun-streaked brown hair that looked as though it would never totally obey a comb.

Weaving through the tables, she was aware of his gaze pinned on what the shirtwaist neatly presented—her slim figure, which, despite its less than willowy stature, offered an arrangement of pleasing contours. All right, so the dress spelled trouble, and she had known that all along.

But so, she realized when she reached him, did his form-fitting knit shirt. She did rather like the breath-catching way it was molded to his broad shoulders and tapered to a narrow waist, and the fact that it was wide open at his bronze neck to expose a triangle of dark, tantalizing chest hair.

His eyes had widened at her approach. They were resting now on the swell of her breasts. She could feel them there, probing. It wasn't easy for her to restrain an embarrassing response to his interest.

"So, there was another Beth Holland under the braid and the baggy blouse."

He would have to go and put it seductively in that lazy, deep drawl of his, she thought. Come on, Beth, be cool about this. Think what experience has taught you in your twenty-seven wise years about how dangerous hunkdom can be. Especially the square-jawed, craggy variety. Hits you right in the gut, that type.

"Apparently another Brian McArdle, too," she said lightly, congratulating herself on her surface aplomb. "What's this in the way of?" She indicated his conservative garb with a casual wave of the hand. "To convince me you're a trustworthy Boy Scout, after all?"

His eyes sparkled. She had the unhappy feeling that she wasn't fooling him at all. "Maybe. Have a seat."

She slid into the booth, and he settled opposite her. The waitress arrived, eyeing Brian's rugged good looks with open admiration as she cleared the table and offered them menus.

Close your mouth, woman. He's only a man. Yes, like Moby Dick is only a whale. Beth smiled at her and shook her head. "Just coffee for me. Black, please. I had a late lunch."

Brian nodded. "The same. I ate on the road coming in."

The waitress departed reluctantly.

Able to sustain her light mood—though it wasn't easy when he leaned toward her to rest a pair of hair-darkened, sinewy forearms on the table between them—Beth asked, "So, what now?"

"We talk a little, and maybe you ask me about my qualifications. You know, the resourceful ones that are going to be useful to you out on that trail."

I know your qualifications, fella, she informed him silently, striving not to sniff the clean, masculine scent that was another result of his metamorphosis. She also tried not to stare at the more obvious portions of the highly appealing physique only inches away from her as she wondered what it would feel like to touch those hard shoulders.

"I don't need to ask," she assured him with an air of nonchalance. *Lord, Beth, you're good.* "Hobart promised me you're reliable when I called them, so I'll go with that. Although—"

The waitress arrived with their coffees.

"Yes?" he prompted when the woman had retreated.

"I still don't understand how you can just pick up like this and be gone for, well, several months at least. I mean, don't you have anyone waiting for you at home?"

His fun-loving eyes were instantly alight with mischief, attractive crinkles deepening at the corners. "Oh, I like that,

Beth. It's your way of finding out whether I'm attached or not. That's cute."

Hunkdom was conceited, too. He didn't deserve an answer. She didn't give him one. She picked up her cup and made a little business of tasting the coffee. It was strong and much too hot. She had trouble not choking on it.

Brian had the decency to look abashed. "Uh...right. To answer your question, there is currently no one private-life-wise who has need of me or claim on me." He sat back in the booth. "Now, have I filled out the application correctly? Do I get the job?"

She set down her cup and pushed it aside, answering him with a shrug. "The choice doesn't seem to be mine. Hobart is insisting on you. But I still don't really understand it. Do I look delicate, incompetent, what?"

"No, you look alone."

She nodded slowly. "I guess it only makes sense not to go alone. Still . . ."

He was leaning toward her again. "Beth, relax, it's going to be fun, I guarantee it."

Relax? When his gaze, as hot as a touch, was assaulting her senses, promising... Well, she didn't dare imagine what those raffish eyes were promising her.

Brian chuckled warmly. "Do you know what you remind me of, sitting there like that with your head tipped over to one side?"

"What?"

"One of those curvy little brown wrens wondering whether it's safe to fly into the feeder."

"Curvy?"

"That's right."

She grinned back at him. "Uh-huh. Just remember, those little wrens are spunky fighters when it comes to having their territories invaded."

"Whoa! Are we about to start the Civil War all over again here?"

"Civil War?"

"You Yankee, me Reb, remember?"

"I hadn't exactly thought of it that way. Interesting analogy."

Brian's eyes were still full of mischief. "Isn't it, though?" He began to drink his coffee.

He could smell her wildflower fragrance from there, and it was damned arousing. *She* was arousing, stimulating areas in him that were already presenting real problems. He had a good mind to back away from this whole thing, pull out now before it got impossibly involved. Someone was apt to get hurt. No, he couldn't do that. There was too much riding on this situation. Besides, the woman intrigued him, provoked feelings in him he couldn't resist. He wanted to know her better.

Beth thought it was time to move on to a safer subject. "If we've covered all that, could we get on to the game plan for tomorrow?"

"You mean like, for starters, how do we get out to this end of the trail?"

"Well, I thought I'd already figured that one. I've garaged my car for the duration and made arrangements to have the local taxi standing by in the morning."

He wiped his mouth with a napkin and lowered his cup. "Now, you see, Beth, here's a case already of where I'm going to be useful to you. Cancel the taxi. We'll use my pickup. I already settled it with a farmer close by the trail on my way in this afternoon. He's agreed to store the pickup for me in one of his sheds."

"That was enterprising of you."

"I'm an enterprising guy, Beth. On a lot of levels."

He never quit, did he? "I believe you. Okay, I'll be waiting for you outside my door at four-thirty."

It was his turn to almost choke. "Four-thirty!"

She laughed at his stunned expression. "We're never going to conquer that trail unless we march out at first light every morning. And we can't even begin to do that until we've driven out to the trail."

He groaned. "And me without any sleep at all last night and that long drive up here."

"I'm sorry. Not going to be so easy being my bodyguard, huh?"

"Not a bodyguard, Beth. A *partner*," he stressed. "There is a difference."

The way he said it, his voice going all soft and husky, had her pulses suddenly racing. Oh, this was awful! How was she going to keep it all business out there on that trail, when he made skyrockets go off inside her every time he—

Beth, stop fighting and go with it. You never know. Given a chance, it just may lead to somewhere warm and wonderful.

The sky was still salted with stars as Beth waited under the fragrant magnolia tree in the motel's parking lot. The early-morning air was damp and chill. It would stay that way until the sun rose, but she was warm enough in her stout hiking shoes, cords and thick camp sweater. Her long chestnut hair was plaited in the heavy braid she always wore when tackling the out-of-doors.

She glanced impatiently at her watch. Drat the man! He was more than twenty minutes late. Where was he? Had he overslept?

Beth would have given anything for a cup of steaming coffee and a toasted English muffin, but in the interest of saving time, she had skipped breakfast this morning. She'd jammed an apple into one of her pockets and she settled for that now, munching on it as she continued to wait restlessly for Brian's arrival.

Her inner grumbling was turning to worry, fear that maybe something had happened to him, when the motel office door behind her opened and the all-night desk clerk stuck her head out, calling a cheerful, "Phone for you, Ms. Holland."

Trouble with that ancient pickup truck of his? Beth wondered as she placed her backpack on the bench outside the door and followed the plump woman into the office. The attendant indicated the phone on the counter and went back to her magazine.

"Where are you?" Beth demanded as she picked up the receiver.

"In Atlanta, where else."

Annie. Beth's heart missed a beat. "Annie, what's wrong? Is it one of the kids? Dick? Has my mother called you trying to reach me?"

"Stop, stop!" her friend's robust voice assured her. "It's nothing like that."

"Then why are you up at this hour calling?"

"Actually, Dick and I are both up with a cranky baby who won't let us sleep when she's in a teething frenzy. But that's beside the point. I wanted to warn you before you headed out, only I was afraid you might have left already, except obviously you haven't. Why?"

"Because Brian McArdle hasn't shown yet, and I didn't remember to ask him where he's staying back in town, so I don't have a number to call him."

There was a thoughtful pause on the Atlanta end before Annie's slow, "Mmm, that figures. May be all part of their strategy."

"Annie, what's this all about? Warn me of what? Have you heard something already?"

"I have. Just a few minutes ago while Dick and I were taking turns trying to soothe Tina, my sweetheart of a husband mumbles, 'Oh, gee, hon, I forgot to tell you what I learned over lunch yesterday.' I could have brained him for not remembering to tell me when he got home last night. I could have called you right then."

"Annie, *what*?"

"This Brian McArdle that Hobart is sending with you. He's not a bodyguard at all, he's a watchdog."

"What does that mean exactly?"

"It means, love, that he isn't there for security purposes. He's there to monitor your hike and report back to Hobart."

Beth could feel a sudden lump of disappointment settling in the bottom of her throat. "A spy! But why?"

"Well, there's a divided camp over that one. According to Dick, half of those in the know think that your watchdog is there to see you're legitimate, that you actually walk the whole trail and don't end up cheating on the hike by getting transport around the tough parts or staying in one place longer than overnight. The other half is betting that he's along to see you *don't* complete the trek by putting little obstacles in your way. What they all agree on is that we're naive if we believe Hobart's one and only concern is your safety, because the word is out that Charles Hobart is really kicking himself for getting into this situation. He doesn't want to see that trail go through his development, Beth."

The lump of disappointment was sinking into her chest, expanding painfully. "I don't believe it! It has to be just speculation, a lot of gossip. Annie, Brian seems so real and honest, not at all like that."

"Beth, he works for Hobart. *They* sent him, and this explains why they're suddenly acting so funny. It's because they're worried you'll find out he's along to check up on you or that you'll learn they're hoping you'll slip up somehow. For all you know, maybe he's already up to his dirty work. Why isn't he there and why did he conveniently forget to tell you where he's staying?" Annie didn't wait for Beth's answer. "Maybe so you get a late start on your first crucial day, that's why. Well?"

"I don't know. I guess it makes sense, except—"

"Yeah, I know, he's gorgeous. And so were a few others you let fool you when you were into causes, remember? My advice is to keep your distance out there. In fact, if I were you, I'd ditch him now while I had the chance. Hey, you mutt, stop that! You're supposed to be housebroken! Beth, I gotta go. The dog's piddling here on the floor, and Dick is hollering it's my turn to comfort our daughter. You keep in touch, and I'll see what else I can come up with. Hey, you okay?"

"I'm okay, Annie."

But Beth didn't feel okay as she left Annie and went out to sit on the bench beside her backpack. She felt deflated. Worse, she felt betrayed. Last night in the coffee shop she had been more than just attracted to Brian. She had begun to see a specialness in him, sense an awakening chemistry between them that had been exciting, making her look forward to this morning, to being with him again.

It would seem, though, that what had dazzled her in the coffee shop had all been an act, that he was merely using her for the sake of his job. Because now, literally in the cold morning light, Beth couldn't deny to herself that from their first contact in her motel doorway, she had felt Brian McArdle wasn't what he pretended to be and that Hobart Development was up to something.

The more she thought about it, the more cheated and angry she felt. Why wasn't he here to defend himself? He was more than just a little late. He was *very* late. If this was all her hike meant to him, then Brian McArdle wasn't very important. The waiting trail was.

Smothering any regrets or remorse, Beth convinced herself that Brian deserved to be left behind. After all, Hobart wasn't playing fair. If they regarded her leaving here without their man as a violation of the agreement, she would remind them of that. She got resolutely to her feet and went into the motel office to call for a taxi.

While she waited for her cab, Beth wrote a quick note of explanation and handed it to the desk clerk. "If Mr. McArdle shows and asks for me, would you give him this, please?"

The pickup had not arrived by the time the taxi appeared and Beth climbed into it, still resisting any last-minute reluctance. But self-control was less easy to maintain as the motel vanished behind her. She was unable to relax and kept glancing around, half expecting to spot the lights of an old pickup truck piercing the darkness as it chased after them. There were never any lights. They were alone on a country highway, no other traffic in sight at this early hour. Brian wasn't following them. She could forget all about him and concentrate on the trail that was waiting for her. Somehow, though, the prospect of a solitary long-distance hike was a less appealing adventure than it had been only yesterday.

The sky was paling, heralding daybreak, when the taxi deposited Beth at the deserted park that was the gateway to the Appalachian Trail. As she slipped into her backpack, the young driver turned the cab, wished her good-luck from the open window and sped away into the dusk. She was suddenly alone in the vast stillness of forest and field.

Might as well get used to it right now, Beth, because from here on out, long weeks to come, you are on your own.

Adjusting the hip belt of the backpack, she struck out on the first of the nearly five million steps needed to take her from Georgia to Maine, a monumental feat if she achieved it. And she had promised herself that she wouldn't quit until she had.

First, she had to gain the official start of the Appalachian Trail, which was not down here but almost four thousand feet above her atop Springer Mountain. It was an arduous challenge in itself but one Beth energetically met by climbing steadily without faltering. Those long hikes over the Mississippi River bluffs back home in Wisconsin had conditioned her for terrain very much like this.

Sunrise caught her on Springer Mountain, and she gasped with pleasure at what the morning light revealed. The whole mountainside was aflame with azaleas, birds singing everywhere in the laurel thickets, the air clean and bracing.

The sun was over the treetops when she reached the bronze plaque proclaiming the southern terminus of the Appalachian Trail. That was when she became aware of something else above the treetops—a helicopter flashing in the sun as it beat toward her.

It was hovering now overhead, and before she could wonder what it was seeking, the noisy chopper settled in a level clearing nearby. Beth couldn't believe her eyes when Brian McArdle emerged from the machine—six feet of dynamic manhood and a cocky grin moving toward her as the helicopter lifted and swam away again over the mountain.

The wild thrill that the sight of him produced was a feeling that Beth permitted herself to experience only briefly. She immediately realized that if Hobart was willing to foot the bill for a hired chopper to deliver this maniac to the top of a mountain, then they would go to any lengths not to lose track of her. The situation only confirmed her worst suspicions about Brian.

"Is this your specialty?" she asked dryly as he joined her. His backpack was in place and he seemed ready for the trail. "Turning up dramatically and unexpectedly?"

"I only make a habit of it with you, Beth." He greeted her with a hearty chuckle. "You have to admit my timing is good on this one. Sorry about the chopper, but it was the only way I could catch up with you. The damn hotel didn't call my room when they were supposed to, and I slept right through our date. I was that tired after two days without sleep."

One more lie I'm feeding her, Brian thought, and he hated himself for it. He could see she was mad. She'd be a lot madder if she knew that the chopper had just brought him from a meeting in Atlanta regarding her. He despised all this subterfuge, the possibility of hurting her. Damn Charles for getting them into this mess!

Brian looked sheepish when her only response was a cool stare. She knew he felt her anger, but he misunderstood it when he said, "Guess you gave up on me when I didn't show, huh?"

"I gave up on you when I learned this morning just what you and Hobart are up to. You're a troubleshooter for them, all right, and I'm the trouble. You've been sent out here to keep me under surveillance, maybe even more than that, for all I know."

He said nothing. So he wasn't going to deny it, she thought. She had expected him to, and a part of her had even hoped he would. But how could he deny what was so obviously true?

"Well?"

He shook his head. "How can I explain to you when you're in this state?"

That meant he didn't have any explanation. Maybe he would come up with one eventually, but she wasn't going to wait for it. Remembering Annie's advice, Beth made up her mind. "All right," she informed him in a cool voice, "it's a public trail. I can't stop you from walking it. But not with me. If you have to do your spying, you can do it from a distance. And if you don't keep back and out of my way, I'll report you for harassment at the first opportunity."

Not waiting for his reaction, Beth turned and swung off through the pines with the stride of a marathon walker.

"Hey, Yank," he shouted after her. "You start off with that kind of gait, you'll drop before you're ever out of Georgia."

She didn't turn her head. She did just what she intended to do from now on—ignore him. But it didn't help her mood to realize that he was right. She had no business long-legging it like a novice. Well, there was always the hope that she could outdistance and lose him.

No such luck. Brian kept her in sight throughout the morning, staying approximately thirty yards behind her, careful not to close the distance between them by slowing his steps whenever she slowed hers, and just as careful not to lose her by speeding up again when she quickened the pace.

Beth knew this because she found herself periodically looking over her shoulder to check his position. She hated herself for her weakness, but she couldn't help it. His presence unnerved her for reasons she didn't care to examine, and she couldn't stand not knowing exactly where he was at all times.

She couldn't have missed him if he'd been a *hundred* yards away. He was wearing another outrageous getup— Argyle socks that would have embarrassed a rainbow, khaki shorts, a woolen lumber jacket in the loudest of plaids and, parked on his thick wayward hair, a rakish panama that Rhett Butler might have envied.

That ought to effectively keep all the wildlife at a safe distance, Beth decided with an unhappy grimace. No question about it. The man was a maverick in every sense of the word.

What was she going to do about him? She couldn't shake him, and he was too smart to give her any real cause for registering a complaint. Though he stuck to her like a burr, he was careful not to acknowledge her existence with any speech or action. Not so much as a nod. Nothing that would constitute a nuisance. He simply strolled along looking as though he were there for no other purpose than to admire the scenery.

Beth decided finally to follow his example and do what she had promised herself she would do—forget about him and enjoy the trail. For a while it worked. The beauty of the Chattahoochee National Forest, which was this portion of the Appalachian Trail, with its carpets of wildflowers and magnificent old trees, was very beautiful. She could almost pretend she was alone in the wilderness.

Almost, because Brian subtly saw to it that she didn't entirely forget about him. Whenever she looked too interested in one of the white blazes that periodically marked the trail or a soothing dogwood on a mossy slope, he would start whistling softly, just to remind her he was still there. He seemed particularly fond of "On the Road Again," which was no doubt a result of his attending country music jamborees.

The provoking situation underwent another subtle change after their lunch break, which consisted of separate cups of instant soup at separate boulders and, of course, no word exchanged. When Beth moved on again, Brian doggedly behind her, she could sense a difference in his interest. He wasn't merely shadowing her this time, he was . . . well, she wasn't sure. But she could *feel* a very pronounced gleam in those blue-green eyes, could spot it, too, whenever she glanced back, even at a distance of thirty yards. It was somehow familiar. And deeply disconcerting.

Suddenly she knew. A fellow naturalist she had once briefly dated used to gaze at her in that same inflammatory way whenever he walked behind her, claiming she had the most alluring bottom of any woman he knew. Brian McArdle was deliberately savoring her backside and relishing the view with every step!

She refused to be aroused in any way by his searing interest. She absolutely *refused*—

Beth came to a halt, whole body clenched in frustration. She couldn't stand this! He was making her a nervous wreck. She had been so convinced that he would tire of his cat-and-mouse game, even give up on her, but there was no sign of that yet and no hope of getting rid of him. Was it to go on like this all the way to Maine?

She had to do something! With those eyes riveted on her, she would end up visibly squirming, and wouldn't he just love that? She wasn't going to provide him the satisfaction.

Mind made up, she turned and communicated with a beckoning finger. He had been waiting patiently back along the path, pretending momentary interest in an ordinary fungus. He was just as obvious now in pretending surprise as he pointed to himself. "Who? Me?"

Beth sighed. "No," she called back, "the crowd behind you." Oh, why did he have to make it harder with this eternal, crazy humor of his? Didn't he feel any shame at all over what he was subjecting her to?

The afternoon had turned warm and humid. As Brian moved up to join her, she noticed that he had shed the lumber jacket, peeling down to a dark blue tank top that disclosed a pair of brawny biceps. He smelled hot and primitively male.

Beth felt woozy from his closeness. She hadn't counted on this. How was she to maintain detachment when she was still so violently attracted to him? She had been convinced that sort of intoxication would vanish with her anger, but it hadn't. She found it hard to breathe suddenly. Maybe it was the close air.

She tried to concentrate on his face when she spoke to him, to ignore his disturbing physical nearness. "I don't like you back there. I feel positively stalked."

He was all innocence. "You don't want me behind you?"

"That's right, I don't want you behind me. If you have to be out here, try walking in front of me for a change. See how *you* like being followed."

"Up there, huh?"

She nodded. "Up there."

"How far up there?"

Preserving self-control, at least on the surface, Beth jerked her thumb along the trail. "Move, please."

"Yes, ma'am."

She gave him the same thirty yards he had given her, and then she started after him.

They proceeded in this fashion less than a mile along the trail, when Beth groaned in defeat. This was no good! This was worse, much worse!

There was no way she could avoid the view straight ahead of her, and that view was utterly demoralizing. Why did he have to be encased in tight shorts like that, have a pair of arousingly muscular bare legs with hairy thighs rippling sensuously as he moved in that easy, masculine stride, and a slim-hipped, male backside that—

Stop it, Beth! You're as bad as he is! You've never let a man affect you this strongly before, and this one is your enemy! So, why him? What's gotten into you?

Now what? Obviously, there was only one safe choice—the one she should have made at the start and would have made if she hadn't been so hurt and angry over his treachery.

Beth came to another halt, calling to him again. "Could you come here, please?"

Three

Brian turned and trotted back to her with an agreeable "What's up?"

"Look, I—I don't like you walking in front of me any better than I like you walking behind me." She hoped he wouldn't demand an explanation for that one. "If you insist on walking this trail at the same time I'm walking this trail, you might as well tramp along beside me. Just don't get any wrong ideas. I still don't consider you with me. Is that clear?"

"I think so. We're going to be covering the trail more or less side by side, but we're not together. Is that right?"

"That's right. And if there's any dialogue, I expect you to keep it strictly impersonal."

"All sounds real logical to me, Beth."

She didn't care whether it made sense to him or not, as long as it worked. He fell into step beside her, and she discovered that the new arrangement did have the advantage she sought. Despite his closeness, she didn't have to look at him directly or be looked at. Unfortunately, she hadn't reckoned with the fact that she would have to listen to him. He proceeded to talk nonstop. The inanities poured out of him.

He had gotten real lonely back there on the trail all those hours. He sure did appreciate this chance for some company. Come on, admit it, hadn't she got a bit lonely herself? Sure she had, and this was much nicer, wasn't it? Not that lonely was all that bad, mind you, when you had marvelous country like this to be lonely in. Actually, he'd been reading up on the trail last night after he left the coffee shop, and it was fascinating. Did she realize, for instance, that the Appalachian Trail passed through a total of fourteen states, eight national forests and six national parks? Amazing, right? And did she also know that this wilderness route was within a mere day's drive of half the population of the United States? His book explained why the National Park Service was so anxious to acquire those last crucial parcels still in private hands, though, of course, it was the Appalachian Trail Conference that actually administered the A.T.

Yes, thank you very much, she did know all that. And just what did this lummox suppose she was doing out here if she *hadn't* already known everything he was so eager to share, which in the next hour was considerable. Well, she had asked for it with that last instruction, and apparently she was getting it.

When he began relating the varieties of wildlife a hiker could expect to encounter on the A.T., Beth could endure no more. She came to an abrupt stop and faced him grimly. "All right, that's it!"

He must have sensed what was coming. He looked and sounded like the ultimate victim. "What have I done now?"

"What have I done now?" She nodded slowly. "The man wants to know what he's done now. Shall we tell him what he's done? Oh, why not? Let's pretend he really doesn't realize that from the beginning he's made a mockery out of this expedition, even though he's been assured its intention is a serious one."

"Mockery? I was just being friendly while keeping it impersonal, like you said. Hey, I'm a Southerner, remember? We like to talk."

"Yes, incessantly. It was either your idea of another bit of cute comedy, or else you really and truly believed I didn't already know that black bears positively adore peanut butter sandwiches and it was your duty to see to it I was provided with this vital information. Just in case I ever ran into a black bear while munching on a peanut butter sandwich, I suppose. Whatever the reason, I didn't want to hear it, just as I don't want to hear all the other recently acquired guidebook wisdom you were no doubt planning to dump on me. I appear to be stuck with you, and since I don't seem to be able to do anything about it at the moment, I would be on-my-knees grateful if you would—if you—if— *You stinker!*"

He was grinning at her. Grinning like a fool. Only he wasn't a fool, she suddenly realized, though he had been playing the fool to his advantage. Oh, she understood that charming grin all right. His nonsense from the start this morning had been deliberate and persistent, calculated to eventually thaw her. Well, it had worked. Unable to sustain her anger, finally recognizing the absurdity of the whole thing, Beth released herself in laughter—a bout of uncontrolled mirth that, after long hours of strain, was pure bliss.

"You feeling better?" he inquired mildly.

She sniffed, then breathed deeply. "Tell me something."

"Sure."

"Are you always so excessive about everything?"

"Only when it gets me somewhere—like cooling you down so I can offer the explanation you weren't about to hear when I joined you this morning."

Beth nodded. "I guess maybe I have been unfair about that. I guess I do owe you the chance to explain. *Have* you got an explanation I could buy?"

"About my being a spy for Hobart?"

"Yes. Make it good now."

He shook his head, leaning back against the trunk of a hemlock. "Can't do it. I am a spy."

"You admit it?"

"Well, sure—except I'd put it in friendlier terms. *Spy* isn't a very nice word, Beth."

"How would you put it?"

"I'd say I'm here on behalf of Hobart to monitor your hike. However it happened, the company has an agreement with you, and since they've got something to lose, you can't expect them to blindly trust someone who walked into their offices out of nowhere. That doesn't mean that they aren't also interested in your welfare, just like I said at the start. Now—reasonable?"

Beth thought about it for a moment. "I guess it is at that," she admitted. "I guess it was naive of me to suppose Hobart wouldn't want the hike checked out by one of their own people. And that's all?"

"That's all. We go on?"

"We go on," she agreed. His argument had been direct and simple, and she could actually appreciate it now. She just wished he had been open about it from the beginning, but it was a relief to have it settled.

He fell into step beside her. "I don't suppose you'd want to tell me how you found out I'm here to monitor your progress?"

Beth didn't want to involve Annie. She kept her eyes on the trail and her mouth closed.

He got the message. "Or maybe not." Silence from him, and then, "Could be, though, there is something you could tell me."

"Like?"

"Is it only the environmental stuff you get this hot and feisty about, or are you into other causes, too? I mean, I just like to know what I'm dealing with here."

Beth smiled. The subject seemed a safe one this time. "Oh, I'm a regular catalog of causes. All the Don Quixote stuff."

"That so?"

"I'm serious. I have absolutely no resistance whenever I see abuses. Been that way ever since I was so high. It's gotten me into more hot water."

"For instance?"

"Well, when I was about eight or nine I met this brokenhearted little boy in a Milwaukee park. Seems his bike had been stolen that morning, and he knew who had it, but nobody would do anything about helping him to get it back."

"And you would?"

"Of course. Even then I knew all about moral outrage. Marched with him right up to the house of the kid who had his bike. I distracted the people at their front door while he slipped his bike out of their garage."

"Good for you."

"Actually, not so good. My wronged boy was a little con artist. Turns out I helped him to snatch a bike that wasn't his. My parents weren't too happy."

"Shocking!"

"It gets worse. When I was in college there was this politician running for national office, and he was concerned about animal rights and Third World hunger. Now, how could I not campaign with a vengeance for somebody like that?"

"Naturally."

"Oh, I really admired that man. Didn't hurt that he was also good-looking."

"What happened?"

"A lech. What is it with some men? Anyway, we were at this rally, and he tried to get cute with me behind the platform—in fact, while his wife was up front speaking on his behalf. Boy, was I ever disillusioned. Fortunately, I was into karate in those days."

"I'll remember that. What else?"

"Well, there were the Florida manatees."

"Don't tell me. You were working to save them."

"Certainly. Only there was this guy who joined our cause, and he— Look, you don't want to hear all this stuff."

"Yeah, I do. It's even better than the scenery. So what about this Florida manatee guy?"

"Okay, how was I to know he was a free-lance journalist who infiltrated our group because he was after a hot story? I mean, he seemed so nice, and I had to share all our inside information with him, didn't I? If he was going to be one of us? What a story *he* wrote! Called us a bunch of bleeding-heart activists. It was really unfair."

"Looks to me, Beth, like you got all your causes mixed up with your men."

His observation startled her a bit, either because she had never fully appreciated until now how true it was or because she couldn't believe she had just confided to him a major vulnerability. "Mmm," she conceded, "I suppose."

Which is exactly why, Brian thought to himself, that you've learned to be wary of men who enter your life. Why you don't trust me. But I want you to trust me, Beth. I find that more and more I want you to trust me.

He eyed her covertly as she moved beside him along the trail. He liked the way the thick braid hanging down her back bounced slightly with each step.

She was obviously a woman with a strong purpose, and he admired the spirit and energy that drove her. But her fight, her direction, was in opposition to his, and there lay the problem. And what could he do about it? When you got right down to it, she was the enemy, and he didn't want her to be the enemy.

And Beth had to keep telling herself that he represented the other side. She had to stop feeling those little glows of pleasure every time he glanced at her. Maybe she shouldn't have shared all that personal stuff. Now he knew she was susceptible.

It had been so easy relating to him, though. As if he really cared. Like a friend.

What have we got here, she wondered. Now he's a friend? That was scary.

But why shouldn't he be a friend? If they could survive with each other.

Just friends. The idea was appealing. It was also a mistake, as she learned several miles later. They were nearing the shelter where she intended for them to camp the first night. At this point the trail crossed a stream in a fern-shrouded ravine. There was no bridge, just stepping-stones around which the cold mountain waters raced. Brian went first and turned to wait for her.

The first stones were easy, but Beth paused on the last boulder to judge the gap that still separated her from the bank. This final reach was too wide for her. She would have to leap it.

Brian outstretched his hand. "Come on, I'll catch you."

Beth shook her head. The idea of physical contact with him . . . well, better not risk it.

"Don't be silly," he urged. "With that thirty-pound weight on your back you'll end up in the drink."

He was right. She was being silly. "All right," she agreed.

She launched herself from the rock—more forcefully than was required, apparently, since she felt herself shooting past his hand and slamming into the hard wall of his chest.

The impact nearly lost him his balance on the slick edge of the stream. In the circumstances, since she was helplessly leaning into him, he couldn't properly recover his equilibrium without recovering hers as well, and that required his arms tight around her waist as he steadied them both.

There she was, like it or not, in his embrace. She *did* like it. Much too much. Of course, that was the whole problem. It had to do with getting jolted into a whole new awareness of him—very disturbing things like the awesome size and power of the body pressed to hers, the heat of a pair of big hands gripping her protectively, the moist and musky closeness of male flesh rapidly costing her her reason. Talk about your savage responses!

There was probably no wisdom in raising her gaze to meet his, but she couldn't help herself. She needed to know his reaction. Yes, big mistake. There was no safe levity now in those killer eyes searching hers, just something long and deep and—what? Well, she didn't know what he could be thinking.

Brian wasn't thinking. He was feeling. Her breasts were crushed against him, a pliant softness that was firing an ache in his gut and a sudden thickening in his loins, and if she went on slowly squirming like that, even if it wasn't intended as an arousal but was merely an effort to extricate herself, then he wasn't going to be responsible for his control.

Beth was being firm with herself by then—something about having no business finding herself in such a situation and that she had this really serious hike to get on with. It did permit her to free herself and step back in safety.

"You all right?" he asked.

"Fine."

"Guess we can move on then."

"Right. Shelter should be just up ahead."

The dialogue was ordinary. As though nothing had happened. Well, that was encouraging.

But Beth couldn't deny that she was shaken by their encounter and was still thinking about it long after they arrived at the camping site. They were to be the only occupants of the crude shelter, though at one point their tranquility was threatened by the noisy arrival of a southbound Scout troop. However, the two leaders decided that the facilities weren't adequate for their numbers, and the pack moved on to a hostel in a nearby village. Serenity returned to the clearing.

Dusk was settling over the forest as Beth sat outside the shelter, watching Brian at the pump washing the metal cups out of which they had eaten their meal of dehydrated beef stew. She had unbound her braid and was making an effort to comb her hair. The hair was too long, impractical for the trail. She ought to have had it cut. Taking care of it out in the open like this every night, not being able to shampoo it regularly, was going to be a real problem.

She dragged the comb through her chestnut waves with impatient strokes, knowing it wasn't her hair that was worrying her. No, she was concerned about what had happened at the stream earlier—and about everything that had preceded it from the moment Brian McArdle came knocking on her motel room door. There wasn't only a sexual current crackling between them, pronounced though that had been from the start. She wasn't a wanton, even if she had felt like one all day. No, if she had to, she was sure she could pull back on that.

The thing of it was, she realized, eyeing the strapping figure at the pump, there were all these other emerging qualities that ultimately counted for a lot more than old-fashioned lust. She had been discovering those qualities in him all day—humor, sensitivity, intelligence—all the good stuff that made a man far more exciting than mere physique. She hoped she wasn't wrong about those qualities. She didn't think she was. And if it came down to it—because she couldn't forget that he was still Hobart's man—this was the Brian McArdle who was going to be tough to resist.

An hour later, tucked inside her sleeping bag on a hard bunk under the shelter, Beth was still fretting as a whip-poorwill called from the forest and was answered by an owl.

"Says you," she muttered.

"Huh?" Brian mumbled sleepily from his own bag across the shelter.

"Nothing," she whispered back. "Go to sleep."

She decided that was very good advice, much more sensible than all this stewing about something that had yet, if ever, to turn really serious. She closed her eyes and went to sleep.

"Howard's Corners!" Brian announced, as thrilled as a kid who'd just made the Little League Majors.

"Howard who?" Beth asked, stirring her breakfast of instant oatmeal in her metal cup.

"Corners," he explained, his finger stabbing at the page of the trail guidebook he had open on his lap as he perched on a corner of the outdoor fireplace. "It's a general store."

"Yes?"

"It's right off the trail up here on a country crossroads. We ought to get there in a couple of hours."

She glanced over his shoulder at the map and listings. "And Howard's Corners is something to be excited about?"

"Well, sure, when it's the genuine article and not one of your touristy pretend things. These hills still have a few old-time general stores in them, and this one is guaranteed. They're fun."

She smiled at him. "Like country jamborees?"

"Yeah, all the down-home stuff. Hey, Beth, I'm just a good ol' boy at heart, you know."

"Uh-huh."

"What's the matter? You've never been inside a real general store?"

"As a matter of fact, I have. We still have a couple of them back in Wisconsin. I can remember my folks taking me to one out in the boonies when I was a kid. I guess they wanted me to see that the whole world doesn't shop in sub-urban supermarkets. It was an education."

"Well, there you go." He snapped the book shut with an expression of satisfaction. "You'll know your way around then when we get to Howard's Corners."

She liked his excitement. There was something heartening about a man who could be pleased over simple things like general stores and country music. "I guess we do need to stock up on a few provisions," she conceded. "Think Howard will have them?"

"Sure to," he promised.

It wasn't a Howard, though, who stood behind the counter of the general store when they reached Brian's discovery well before midmorning. The woman wore a Dolly Parton wig, chewed gum and greeted them with a warm, "Well, hey there!"

Brian leaned his elbows on the counter and proceeded to charm her. Beth could have sworn that his mellow Georgia drawl unconsciously deepened. He was wonderful with people, relating to them with ease. She had seen that last night at the shelter when he talked to the two Scout leaders.

Easy, Beth. Start finding some flaws. You know, just in case.

It seemed wiser at this point to turn away from the counter. She left the two of them chatting and began to wander through the store. She could immediately see that Brian wouldn't be disappointed when he finally tore himself away from the counter and got around to exploring the contents of Howard's Corners. It was all there: fat barrels along the wooden floor of crowded aisles, dusty glass cases, sickly jade plants stuffed in unlikely corners, potbellied stove in the middle, even the mysterious and authentic odors associated with everyone's image of a general store. Forget that a modern freezer case stretched along one wall.

Beth wound up back at the counter, asking, "Is there a public phone I could use?" It was time to check in with Annie.

"Sure is, missy. You passed it out there along the porch."

She left Brian happily chasing down the treasures of Howard's Corners and went out to make her call.

She thought for a second she'd dialed the wrong number when the receiver was snatched up at the other end and a voice snarled in her ear, "This is it! I'm filing for divorce! I get the house, *you* get the kids!"

"Annie?"

"Beth! Oh my gosh, I'm sorry! I was in the middle of a muddle here when Dick called from his office. He said he'd ring back in five minutes, and I thought—"

"Anything serious?"

"Just the usual small-fry battles plus the damn dog throwing up his morning snack on my clean kitchen floor. If I'd been smart, Beth, I would never have gotten married! That way I'd only have the dog to deal with."

Knowing how much Annie loved her family, Beth wasn't troubled by her friend's irreverence. "Look, maybe I'd better let you go and call back later when it's more convenient."

"Don't worry. I've got a cease-fire here at the moment. I've been hoping you would call. I need to talk to you. Did the watchdog ever show up?"

"Yes."

"And you didn't send him packing?"

"No."

"I was afraid of that. I've got news about him."

Beth wasn't sure she wanted to hear it. She didn't like the drama in Annie's voice.

"He's not just a spy, Beth," Annie went on. "He's what I worried he might be. A saboteur!"

"He's what?"

"It's true. Trust me on this one. It comes from a good source."

"You're telling me that for sure Brian McArdle is out to sabotage my hike? How?"

"Now, Beth, I know you're going to want to shut your ears to this, but just listen to me. It seems this character of yours has got a reputation here in Atlanta with women. I mean, he's practically notorious."

"Because women go for him? That's not his fault, and it's not surprising. Anyway, what's that got to do with—"

"He's there to weaken your defenses. Do I have to draw a picture, or do you see what I mean?"

Beth thought laughter might be appropriate at this moment, but it never surfaced. "Oh, Annie, come on! You're saying that Brian was sent out here to deliberately romance me? That I'm supposed to fall for him so hard I'll be ready to give up the hike if he asks? That isn't just farfetched, it's crazy."

"Well, Beth, think about it. It's really not so crazy if you think about it. Why would a man who's of value to the company—which he must be from what we know—join you out there for a whole three months or better, be gone from his work that long? Just to look out for you, maybe monitor the hike? I don't think so. I think it's because your Hobart Company has something to lose they don't want to lose, and they mean not to lose it. And why pick *him* in particular to send?"

"Because he was available, I suppose."

"Or maybe because he's a hunk that women do fall for. Hey, it's not so farfetched. This kind of sexual subversion has been pulled before, you know."

"Annie, I just don't feel—"

"All I'm saying is that there might be something else there to watch out for. It can't hurt to watch yourself. Listen, remember back at Camp Sweetwater when you thought that John Fierstein was so wonderful, and I tried to tell you he was just using you because you were the only one of us counselors who had a car, and he wanted to borrow it so he could drive into town to see that busty redhead, and it turned out I was right? Remember that?"

"Annie, I was seventeen. And it wasn't John Fierstein. It was Guy What's-his-name."

"Makes no difference. The point is, you're too trusting about guys, and the worst of them seem to sense that and zero in on you, and you wind up getting hurt. For all we know, the Hobart outfit could have learned that about you and decided to use it against you."

Well, if they didn't know, Beth thought with the first stirrings of unease as she remembered her confessions to Brian yesterday, then they certainly do now. This was too wild! Annie had to be wrong on this one!

"Beth, I don't like your silence. Have you gone soft on that guy already?"

"No." *Have I?*

"Well, don't. Even if it ends up he's okay, which I doubt, you can't afford the distraction. This hike is turning out to be too important. People are getting very interested in it back here, Beth. The publicity could really heat up over this issue."

"Annie, go easy on that, will you? I don't want this thing turning into a carnival."

"You want the support, don't you?"

"Yes, but—"

"Relax, I'll handle it. You just walk. I'd better go. Dick is probably trying to reach me. Keep in touch now. You never know what I might hear next."

Which is exactly what I'm worried about, she thought. But she didn't tell Annie that.

Beth was turning from the phone when Brian appeared on the porch. "I picked out what I thought we might need and left it on the counter. Why don't you look it over, and I'll join you in a minute? Got a call of my own to make."

Hobart? she wondered. And what would he tell Atlanta about Beth Holland? That the progress there was favorable? Favorable how?

"All right," she told him cheerfully, turning away before he could see that she wasn't lighthearted at all but uncomfortable suddenly, and that she was unable to meet his gaze because she was ashamed of her suspicions about him.

This was silly! Annie had to be wrong. She wasn't that lousy a judge of a man's character. Experience and maturity had to have taught her something, and when she remembered how Brian was with people, how he cared—well, he wouldn't pull something so rotten as to try to make her fall for him just to sabotage her plans. Wait a minute! She was forgetting something here. Hadn't he already deceived her about why he had come on the hike? Yes, but did that make him capable of deliberately using a woman in the sexual sense because his company was actually paying him to use her?

Her mind wouldn't quit on the subject, and when Beth and Brian regained the trail minutes later, she realized something. What she knew about Brian had to do with impressions, not real knowledge. And without knowledge, she was unable to determine whether there was any substance in Annie's allegation. So, okay, maybe the time had come to learn more about her trail partner.

How do you do that, Beth? Go and ask him?

Why not? "Oh, by the way, would you mind telling me all about your love life? And while you're at it, separate your long parade of women into those you might have cared a little something about and those you cheated for the sake of good old Hobart."

So it was a dumb idea, not the kind of thing you could directly ask a man without sounding like a perfect nitwit, never mind arousing every suspicion in the book. But maybe a little subtle probing when the moment was right? Sure, nothing unnatural in wanting to know a bit more about someone you were going to spend weeks with on a wilderness trail.

The opportunity presented itself at their midmorning break. They found a crude bench on a high rocky overhang and settled on it side by side. There was a purpose in the bench's location since it commanded a spectacular view off to the east—the rolling Blue Ridge Mountains clad in a faint mist, their slopes thick with tangles of wild rhododendron soon to burst into riotous bloom.

Brian produced a paper bag and offered it to her. "Loot from Howard's Corners."

"What is it?"

"Candy."

Beth shook her head without bothering to investigate the contents of the bag. "No, thank you. I try to eat natural foods, especially on the trail like this where fitness counts. You know, nuts and raisins."

"Uh-huh." His big hand dug into the bag.

She watched a handful of licorice bits travel temptingly to his mouth. The rat! How did he guess she was practically addicted to licorice? She watched him chew happily for several seconds, and then she could no longer stand it. "Oh, to hell with health! Pass me that bag."

He grinned at her broadly, handing her the bag.

"Well, licorice is my one weakness in the candy department," she admitted. She helped herself to a generous handful of the bits.

They sat in silence, munching and enjoying the view. An elderly couple with binoculars in hand, obviously out for a morning of bird-watching, passed the bench and nodded at them with friendly smiles.

"Think they noticed our black tongues?" Brian wondered with a rumble of laughter as the couple passed down the trail.

"What?" Beth asked. She had been nervously trying to figure out how she was going to bring herself to ask him what she wanted to ask him.

He turned to her. "You seem a little distracted since we left the store. What's the matter? Upsetting phone call?"

He was giving her an opening. It was time. Beth took a deep breath and plunged.

Four

———

Sorry," she told him with what she hoped was a carefree smile. "Did I give the impression something was bothering me? Actually, I was just thinking. The call was to a friend. She's taking care of some things for me while I'm gone."

Careful, Beth. Go easy with this. The distinctive blue-green eyes were looking into hers. She had the feeling that they were able to read her every emotion, if not her actual thoughts.

"Anyway," she went on lightly, "she happened to ask about you. You know, who you were, what you were like, that kind of thing. Just the usual curiosity."

"What did you tell her?"

"Not much. What did I know to tell her if I wanted to tell her something?"

"And that's what you were thinking about?"

"Exactly. It doesn't seem fair, does it? I mean, after yesterday you know quite a bit about me, but what do I really know about you? If we're going to be traveling together like this for weeks on end..."

"Naturally." Did she detect a dryness in his response, or was she simply being paranoid about this oh-so-nonchalant inquisition of hers? "So, what do you specifically want to know, other than I'm thirty-four, reasonably solvent, and still have all my teeth?"

"Oh, I don't know. Just things, I guess."

"You don't mean 'just things,' Beth. You mean who are the women in my life, and are any of them hanging around right now, and do I care? Just like I wanted to know yesterday about the men in your life."

His male complacency deserved a flaming indignation, but how could she be outraged when he was prepared to tell her just what she wanted to know? At least he wasn't guessing yet *why* she wanted to know. Let him think the worst. Her pride could take it.

"Okay," she admitted. "So I'm obvious. Just don't get the wrong idea about it. Why wouldn't I want to know? You told me in the coffee shop the other night you weren't attached, but that doesn't mean there isn't someone special waiting back there, and if there is... well, it's a little awkward then, our being out here together, don't you think?"

"*Currently* attached," he corrected. "I had a wife once."

"Oh. I'm sorry."

"Why? Trudy isn't. I'm not."

"What happened?" *Other women maybe. The wicked reputation Annie is trying to sell me.*

"The usual. Our life-styles clashed. I liked Willie Nelson, she liked Brahms."

"I see." For a man who seemed pretty sensitive about important things, she thought he was being oddly flippant on the subject of his ex-wife. She wondered why. Or was she just imagining it?

"So there's nobody special back there at the moment. Unless you count my mother. What about you? Anyone serious since the little con artist in the Milwaukee park?"

"Not really. There were a couple of times when I thought, well, maybe . . ." She shook her head. "But, no, it somehow never got to the let's-set-up-house-together stage."

"I remember. They ended up disillusioning you."

Deceiving you, actually, Brian thought. Just like I'm deceiving you now, not giving you the whole truth, the truth that matters, anyway.

He knew what she really needed to know, even if she didn't, and he was withholding it for the sake of the company. Damn it all, he hated this subterfuge, hated putting her through this! But what choice did he have? Hobart's cash flow was tight, its credit strained. It was critical that this Maine development go without a hitch come autumn. Without it, Hobart could sink, and he couldn't risk that. Too many people were involved. Charles should be strangled for bungling this thing. That arrogance of his had gone and dismissed this woman as incapable when she was anything but. His error could hurt all of them.

Beth sat on the bench and watched the play of light and shadow across the farmland in the valley below as lazy clouds came and went over the face of the sun, thinking to herself: This isn't getting me anywhere. Yes, now I know a little more about him than I did before, but it's not telling me whether the man is capable of some devious assault on my libido in order to try to defeat this hike. And I'm not going to find out that kind of thing either by playing games.

Should she come right out and ask him, then? Was she back to that? No, if there was any truth in Annie's claim, he'd only deny it.

This was really stupid! Hobart wasn't going to employ some calculated sexual campaign that was supposed to have her so swooning with ecstasy she'd be begging to give up her hike. No company could be that juvenile.

That was what she thought before she turned to him, ready with the suggestion that it was time they moved on. When she saw the way he was sitting there, looking impossibly confident, jeans-clad legs casually spread, every line of his body boasting his robust male endowments, and when that sight made her go weak all over, Beth wasn't quite so ready to dismiss her apprehension.

Better safe than sorry, she told herself.

From now on she had to protect herself, look for any signs that he might be getting deliberately cute with her, and at all costs avoid another tempting contact like yesterday's. She hated this, but what choice did she have? She didn't trust him, and she didn't trust herself. She would have to watch both of them religiously.

They picked up the trail again. Whenever Brian spoke to her or moved too close on the narrow forest path, Beth tensed, fearing an overture to intimacy. She knew she was overreacting again. The poor man never touched her, never discussed anything more threatening than the beguiling scenery or the distance to their next campsite. He couldn't help it that his solid nearness had the worst kind of effect on her or that his husky drawl, even with his most innocent comments, seemed to stroke the words for her, conveying the wildest possibilities. Well, she couldn't help her wariness, either, though she did finally relax her guard enough to restore her enthusiasm for the trail.

By late morning, however, Beth's feet demanded another time-out. When she spotted the inviting gleam of sun-licked waters through the trees off to the left, she proposed a rest stop. There was a side path that promised to lead them to the water's edge.

"Sounds good," he agreed. "Lead on, Hiawatha."

She plunged down the threadlike trail ahead of him. On its lower reaches grew a thicket of willows, their branches arching tightly over the path. Beth crouched low and worked her way through the tunnel, emerging on the rocky shore of a small lake.

For a moment she was so caught up in the green enchantment of the place she didn't notice that Brian wasn't beside her. She looked around for him then, mystified by his absence.

"I could really use some help." His call came from behind her in the woods.

"Where are you?"

"Back in the willows."

"What are you doing there? The lake's down here."

"Would you mind coming here and finding out, please? Right away, please."

She turned and worked her way back through the close willows, encountering him midway in the thicket. He was hunched over at an awkward angle in an attitude of immobility, his mouth stretched in a tight grimace.

"What have you done to yourself?"

"Not me. This." One finger poked in the general direction of his head and shoulders.

She saw it then. A length of fishing line had been caught in the willows and it had ensnared him as he tried to pass. The malevolent black thread had managed to loop and twist itself in a series of snarls and tangles over his panama hat, around his neck and through the frame of his backpack. He was trussed up like a parcel.

Beth was impressed. "Oh, my. It must have taken genius to get yourself wound up like that."

"It wasn't easy. I'd like to meet the fisherman who cut this vicious thing loose here."

"I don't suppose it occurred to you to just bend over like I did when you came through. That way you would have avoided it."

"May I point out to you that my bending isn't at the same height as your bending? Are you going to help me, or are you going to stand there and discuss it while I slowly strangle?"

"I'm considering the problem. It's very interesting."

"Enjoying yourself, Beth?"

She was, actually, but under the circumstances she didn't think he would appreciate any facial evidence of that. She went, instead, for an expression somewhere between forbearance and mild sympathy. "Hold on while I get out my knife. Where is yours, by the way? Or didn't you consider that you could use it to just cut yourself free?"

"I did, but I couldn't reach around to the pocket in my backpack to get at the damn thing. Every time I tried I was in danger of being garroted by the fishing line or having my neck sliced through from behind by what feels like a nasty fishhook."

Beth had removed her own all-purpose Swiss army knife from her pack. Before using it to extricate him from the line, she examined the back of his neck. "What hook? I don't see any."

"It's there. Right about here." He reached for her hand, intending to guide her fingers up to the area of the fishhook. Remembering her promise to herself to avoid all physical contacts, even innocent ones, Beth removed her hand from the danger zone with a quick, "Never mind. I can see it now under the willow leaves. It's one of those mean, three-pronged jobbies, too."

"Would be. Hurry up. This is not pleasant."

"I will as soon as I figure out where to begin. The stuff is like a web."

"I know. Every time I tried to work myself out of it, all I did was make it worse."

Beth began cutting the line in several spots. "Hold still! You're squirming all over the place!"

"Can't help it. There are gnats zeroing in on my face."

"Stop batting at them. You're only making this harder. There, that ought to do it."

Freed from the line, Brian sighed with relief. "Thank you, and may I never have to return the favor in kind."

"Don't mention it. I'm experienced when it comes to freeing dumb animals from traps. What is it now?"

He had the panama off his head and was worriedly fingering the back of his neck. "I knew it. One of those barbs did pierce me. I'm bleeding."

"Here, let me see." He lowered his head, presenting the back of his neck for her inspection. "Don't be such a baby. It's just a scratch."

"Scratches from fishing hooks can get infected."

Beth issued a long sigh. "Did anyone ever tell you that you're major trouble?"

"Frequently. Do I get treatment or not?"

"Hang on while I clean this up." She found the first-aid kit in her pack, produced the tube of antiseptic cream and uncapped it.

Brian was once again offering the back of his head. Beth had a dab of cream on the end of her finger and was ready to apply it when she thought better of her action. This could amount to another of those intimacies she had sworn to avoid. Just above the nick, his unruly brown hair was damp from the humidity of the day, curling on the nape of a strongly corded, deeply tanned neck. Beth caught her breath. She had never before considered that a male neck could be sexy, but this one was. She wasn't going to touch that warm flesh, even if the situation wasn't intentional on his part.

"Here." She shoved the tube into his hand. "You're a big boy. You can take care of your own wound. I'll wait for you at the lake."

She turned and made her way back to the shore. When he joined her moments later, he found her settled on a flat boulder at the lake's edge. She had removed her shoes and double layer of socks and was cooling her burning feet in the sweet waters of the lake.

"Great," he pronounced. "Mind if I join you?"

"There's no charge. How's the boo-boo?"

"Out of intensive care." Within seconds, he was seated beside her on the boulder, jeans rolled up, and happily lowering a pair of large bare feet into the waters. "Ahh...nice, huh?"

"Nice," she agreed.

They sat there companionably, shoulder to shoulder, for a quiet minute. Beth was just managing to relax, to persuade herself that maybe she was being irrational trying to maintain this guard against him at every turn, when Brian observed with a nod in the direction of her hiking shoes, "I wouldn't count on those making it to Maine, Beth."

She came sharply out of her reverie. "What does that mean?"

"They look like they have light-years on them."

Why did he have this talent for getting to her? All he had to do was look at her, and either her senses started swimming or she became ready to fight. Well, maybe fighting was safer.

"They're just well broken in," she informed him crisply, "which was very smart of me. They'll make it all right, maybe with a little repair before the end, but they'll make it. And stop picking on my hiking shoes. If we're going to pick on something, we ought to start with that hat of yours.'' She indicated the wide-brimmed, low-crowned panama resting on the boulder beside him.

"And what's wrong with my hat?''

"It's awful. Where do you think you are? On safari?''

"Listen, this is not affectation. It's a valuable asset. Now, just look.'' He picked up the panama and began to point out its merits. "The straw allows it to breathe, see, and that makes it cool. At the same time, the wide brim keeps the hot sun off my head, and this band...this band right inside here, that absorbs the perspiration. Useful, right?''

"Uh-huh. So useful it was probably what snagged that fishing line in the first place. And *don't*—'' she held up one hand as his mouth opened for a rebuttal ''—let's go on arguing about it. Whose fault is it, anyhow, that we got into this?''

She stared at him, he stared at her. *"Yours!"* they answered simultaneously and found themselves breaking into long laughter.

Brian stuck out his hand. "Truce, Yank?''

Beth was so caught up in the mirthful moment that she didn't hesitate. "Truce, Reb.'' She clasped his hand with her own.

They shook briefly, but when she went to withdraw her hand, he clung to it, his forefinger slowly rubbing across the pulse point at the back of her wrist, sending a wild current racing through her body.

Beth snatched her hand away in alarm. She wasn't imagining it this time. He was wearing a playful smile, but whatever his motive, his action had been deliberate, intended to undermine her defenses.

No more weak moments, Beth, she reminded herself. From now on, you stay alert. Hear? And don't let him see that he affected you with that sneaky little performance, either.

Turning away from him, she lifted her feet from the water, reaching for her shoes and socks. "Come on, Reb," she ordered, bringing the mood back to a safe lightness. "Let's hit the trail before I have to go and rescue you from something else."

"Not fair," he said, hunting for his own socks. "We're supposed to be a team here, remember? Maybe your turn is coming up."

"Oh, I wouldn't count on that."

Beth was to regret her boast before the day ended.

By midafternoon, the temperature and humidity had climbed. The heavier air seemed to bring out all the tangy, woodsy smells of the forest. Unhappily, it also brought out the mosquitoes. In force.

Beth was prepared. Securing the repellent from her pack, she dampened herself liberally before offering the package of towelettes to Brian.

"No thanks," he refused airily. "Never use it."

"Fine. Be eaten alive then."

A quarter of a mile down the trail Beth was still swatting, slapping and suffering. "I don't understand it," she grumbled. "The stuff always worked like magic before."

"Wisconsin mosquitoes, Beth. The Southern ones are meaner."

"Nothing is meaner than a North Woods mosquito."

But the fact remained, the repellent failed to discourage the persistent devils. They were feasting on her regularly by now. Equally puzzling and irksome was her companion's apparent immunity. Brian had changed into shorts and a tank top again during the lunch break. Acres of healthy, muscled flesh were invitingly exposed. The mosquitoes seemed uninterested, preferring Beth. Brian swung along beside her in perfect contentment.

"I don't get it," she said, waving off her attackers. "Gnats bother you, mosquitoes don't?"

"I'm selective about my insects, Beth."

"Come on, what's your secret? What are you using to keep them off?"

"My sense of humor."

"All right, be a smart aleck."

"No, it's true. Word of honor."

She stopped on the path, head tipped to one side as she considered him with a this-one-ought-to-be-good expression.

Brian grinned down at her. "There's that suspicious little brown wren again."

"The wren is going to regret this, but, come on, let's have it and get it over with. Sense of humor, huh?"

"That's right. Well, more or less. See, if you're relaxed and having fun and not being uptight about everything that comes along, then certain insects, like mosquitoes, don't seem to be attracted. What attracts them is a lot of adrenaline in the bloodstream that comes from being intense. Scientific fact."

"I see. So what you're telling me is that you're okay because you're jumping for joy while I'm being drained here because I'm too intense. Is that it?" She endeavored to mash the mosquito currently settled on the back of her neck as inconspicuously as possible in order not to add support to Brian's wacky theory.

"Don't know, Beth, but it looks to me like you have been kind of intense ever since Howard's Corners."

He was far too observant. Maybe he was trying to find out just what she had learned in her phone call. That was something else now she would have to look out for.

"So, what do you think?"

"What do I think? I think you are full of you-know-what. Absolutely scientific you-know-what, of course. And I am not intense."

He met her challenging gaze with a warm chuckle. "Okay, so I don't know why the mosquitoes leave me alone, but it figures it's got something to do with body chemistry, right?"

At that point, Beth really didn't care. She was too busy fending off the insect population, which seemed to be intensifying its assault with every step she took.

After a minute, watching her increasing misery as they moved on, Brian offered mysteriously, "I can help if you'd like. I know a surefire protection."

The temptation to be rescued was considerable, but Beth feared his cure might involve touching. Besides, after her boast this morning, it was a matter of pride to stubbornly resist his help. "No, thank you. I'm sure we'll walk out of this bug zone before long."

They didn't. Finally, when she could stand it no longer, she gave in, not caring about the risk. "All right, I admit I'm licked. What is this prescription of yours?"

"Coming right up." He stopped on the path and slung his backpack to the ground, squatting beside it to poke through its contents.

"What's that?" she asked suspiciously as he came up with a fistful of something.

"Two elastic sweatbands and a piece of netting."

"Always come fully prepared, do you?"

"That's me."

Concern mounting, she watched him unfold the sweatbands and netting. "What do you intend doing with those?"

"Just hold still."

"Wait, I don't want you to—"

Too late. He had moved in close to her and was fitting the pair of sweatbands around the crown of her head, one atop the other. She was acutely aware of his nearness, of the heat and bigness of him. His hands were strong and confident, but the lean fingers were making an excessive amount of contact as he arranged the sweatbands, performing what felt more like caresses than simple adjustments.

Beth felt herself tighten with panic. This was it, plain evidence of Annie's assertion that Brian was out to conquer her with every sensual weapon at his disposal, purposefully creating one little crisis after another in order to wear her down. No, that was crazy! He had hardly invented the fishing line or the mosquitoes. All the same, he seemed to be taking advantage of these situations.

If this is a seduction siege, Beth, there is a simple way to withstand it. Just don't visually respond to it. Don't let him see that he's got you where he wants you, and maybe he'll get discouraged and lay off. Control your breathing now and for Pete's sake, stop wiggling.

What the hell is the matter with her today? Brian wondered. She's as jumpy as a grasshopper every time I come anywhere near her. Just what had she heard in that phone call, anyway, to make this change in her? Before that, he could have sworn she was beginning to trust him, and if he could just win that trust—

"What's taking you so long?" Beth demanded, regretting the betraying hoarseness in her voice.

"Relax. You need the thickness of the two sweatbands. Otherwise, the panama will slide right down over your face."

"Oh, no! You're not going to make me wear that hat of yours."

"Told you it was real useful, Beth." He had the panama off his head and was ready to place it on hers. "So, what's it to be? Mosquito meal or swallowed pride?"

She sighed. "Go ahead."

The panama hat was settled on her head, the nylon netting drawn down over it around her face and tucked inside her shirt. For obvious reasons, Beth insisted on securing the netting herself. Brian didn't object, and she felt easier now that she was able to draw away from him.

"Got a pair of gloves in your pack?" he asked.

"Yes. I figured I might need them when I got into the New England mountains."

"Put them on and roll down your shirtsleeves. You're going to be warm, but at least you'll be fairly mosquito-proof."

When no more skin was left exposed, she faced him with a mournful "I must look a sight. Just how bad is it?"

He cocked his head to one side, considering her. "Bee-keeper," he decided with a wicked grin.

They camped that evening in a clearing among pungent-smelling pines where they found safe water for bathing and refilling their canteens. Brian cooked their supper—a freeze-dried version of Southern ham and beans—over one of the tiny butane stoves they both carried, even handling the cleanup afterward.

Beth didn't object. He still seemed remarkably fresh, and she was frankly tired after the stresses of the long day, the least of them being an ornery fishing line and hordes of vicious mosquitoes. It was a wearing process maintaining defenses against a man as physically and emotionally arousing as Brian McArdle, and she was beginning to wonder how much longer she could hold the trenches.

The solid masses of the soaring pines and the long, peaceful spring twilight should have been restful. But Beth couldn't seem to settle her mood as she sat cross-legged on the ground, combing the bodies of dead mosquitoes out of her tumbled hair. Mercifully, with the cooler air, the live ones appeared to have retreated for the day. However, the length of her hair, and all that it insisted on catching on the trail, was proving to be a daily handicap.

When the comb snagged in the chestnut masses, breaking several teeth, she put it down in disgust, sat there for a long reflective moment and then impulsively decided that it had to be done.

When Brian returned from his cleanup, he found her rummaging determinedly through her pack. "What's happening?" he asked.

From the depths of the lower compartment, Beth found and extracted scissors and a pocket mirror. "I'm going to cut my hair."

"You're chopping off all those sexy tresses?" he lamented.

"Every last one of them. I thought it would be all right with the braid on the trail, but the length is still a nuisance. I want it short and manageable." She found a towel and arranged it around her shoulders. "Come on, you're going to help."

He squatted on the ground, facing her. "What do I get to do?"

"You get to hold the mirror for me. Exciting?"

"Best offer I've had today." He picked up the mirror, turning it over in his hand and shaking his head. "Not good, Beth. This thing is a scrap. You'll never see enough of your head at one time to do it properly."

"No choice."

"Yes, there is."

"What?"

"I'll cut it for you."

"No thanks."

"Come on, trust me. I cut everybody's hair in the dorm all through college. They saved money, and I earned money. I got to be real good at it, style and everything. You'll love it."

She gazed at him with uncertainty. He nodded back slowly.

Don't be a fool, she told herself. This kind of thing involves contact. What could she be thinking to even consider it? But he was only cutting her hair. That should be all right, shouldn't it?

She handed him the scissors and comb with a small sigh. "I must be a masochist. Every time you say, 'trust me,' I wind up regretting it. Go ahead. Just one thing, though."

"What?"

"Be kind, will you? I want easy-care, not bald."

"Relax."

"Easy for you to say. You're not the one risking a butchering. Oh, well, if it's too awful, it will have grown out again before I see Maine and a decent mirror."

She hunched there on the ground with a nervous grimace as Brian, up on his knees now, closed in with scissors and comb. She shut her eyes as he began to snip, and she could feel her tresses recklessly falling.

"What are you doing now?" she demanded.

"Tapering the sides and shaping the back. Hold still, will you?"

"Sorry."

When he had shortened the front, Beth could stand it no longer. "Let me have the mirror. I want to see." She peered into the glass as he held it, turning her head from side to side. She was impressed. He had given her a professional-looking cut, carefree and casual and yet attractive. "Not bad. This gets you an A plus, McArdle."

He put down the mirror and leaned in close for a better look. "I'm not sure."

"Oh, but it seems—"

"The front may need a little trimming still. Let me see."

Before she could stop him, his big hands reached out to frame her face on either side. His touch generated an instant, all-too-familiar response. She was quivering like a tuning fork. She tried to draw back, but his long fingers tightened as he slowly tilted her head from side to side, his deep eyes solemnly inspecting her.

"You have the most interesting little dent at the end of your nose," he observed with a soft, lazy huskiness. "I've been watching it all day."

She wanted to be glib in her reply. It seemed the safest thing to be at this point. But glibness wasn't easy when her breathing was so unsteady. "And you have a small scar right there over your left eyebrow. Football maybe?"

"Soccer."

"Oh. Where does all that leave us?"

His voice thickened. "I don't know, Beth. Where does it leave us?"

"What—" she swallowed, fought for a control that was fast slipping away "—has all that to do with hair?"

"What hair?" he wondered.

"I—I don't know," she croaked. How could she know when she was so mesmerized by those smoldering blue-green eyes holding hers like an embrace?

Seconds flew by before his desire-roughened voice slowly asked, "What were you saying?"

Her own voice sounded faint and faraway. "I don't remember."

"Yes, you do," came his challenging whisper. "You were saying, 'We have to do something about this.'"

A siren went off in her head. You're about to commit suicide here, Beth! Get out of this! Now!

She meant to free herself from both his hands and his tight, spellbinding gaze. But the intention required resistance, and the resistance wasn't there. She was without will as he drew her to her knees, his mouth lowering to find hers.

His kiss was a volatile mixture of fire and honey, rocking her senses. She was filled with his woodsy male aroma, the clean, sharp taste of his parted mouth as his lips moved over hers. He deepened the kiss, his arms pulling her against his solidness and his tongue sliding between her teeth to tease and abuse her sanity. She shamelessly exulted in his onslaught, since her senses were already destroyed. No one had ever kissed her like this, with such thoroughness and abandon. She couldn't breathe, could feel her bones turning to heavy, warm liquid as his splayed fingers against her back pressed her into his hardness, wanting her being absorbed with his. Her sensitized breasts swelled against him, their buds hardening, aching, while his skillful tongue went on stroking the depths of her mouth. It wasn't enough. His urgent lips had to be elsewhere then—caressing her eyes, searing her throat, capturing the lobe of her ear.

What was he doing to her?

This couldn't go on! This frightening wildness had to stop!

Sanity fought its way back to the surface, and Beth managed to struggle out of his arms and thrust him away. Weak and shaken, senses still flaring, she issued a raspy, "Please...no more!"

She could see that he had been equally affected. The residue of his arousal was evident in his eyes, dark and hot, in breathing that was still ragged. All the same, he was handling it much better than she was, able after gazing at her silently for a long minute to ask in his easy drawl, "What's wrong?"

What's wrong? She wanted to laugh. Or cry. Maybe both. Everything is wrong, that's what's wrong.

How had this hike, which had started out as a straightforward, worthy challenge, gotten so complicated? No, that wasn't true. The hike wasn't confused, she was. She didn't know what to trust, Annie's insistent accusation or Brian's traumatizing kiss. It couldn't have been just a performance, that fierce, fervent kiss. No one was that good an actor. But there was no way to be sure, and she couldn't take the chance of being wrong. Too much was riding on the outcome of the hike and, now, it seemed, the state of her heart.

What was she going to do? She couldn't take another day like today. She hadn't the energy to both walk the trail and resist his lovemaking, and until she could decide for certain whether he was genuine or simply Hobart's instrument...

He was waiting for her response. She had to tell him something. "Brian, I can't deal with this. It's too fast. I need time to...to get to know you better." It was a lame plea but the best she had to offer.

He shifted, easing his long body back onto the cushion of pine needles. "How much time?" he asked bluntly.

"I don't know." She spread her hands in a gesture of helplessness. "A few days, maybe a week. Just no more close encounters until...oh, you know."

Did he? She couldn't tell. He lay stretched there on the bed of pine needles, gazing up at her impassively. She didn't know whether he was angry, understanding or simply indifferent.

"All right," he promised solemnly. "I won't push it."

But it wouldn't be easy, he knew. His vitals were still suffering the sharp, deep frustration that had wrenched him when she had freed herself from his arms. He wanted to make love to her, and he would have, right out here in the open on the raw earth, if she had let him. He longed for that more than he had ever longed for anything, but it wouldn't be any good unless she wanted it as much as he did.

With her history, she wouldn't want it until she fully trusted him. Beth Holland wasn't going to be easy. And he didn't want her to be. With a sudden sense of wonder, he realized that this woman was beginning to matter more than she was supposed to matter. What was happening here? Maybe he needed a time-out as much as she did. Okay, but how was he supposed to stand being near her and not touch her? Restraint, McArdle, he cautioned himself. Massive restraint. It's worth it, if, in the end, it makes all the difference.

A new moon was rising through the pines, the night humming with insects, as Beth crawled into her sleeping bag a half hour later. She could still feel the impact of Brian's mouth on hers, branding her, and the sensation was frightening.

This could be serious! This was no ordinary man and no ordinary connection she had with him. There was the potential here for something deep and very, very intense. If something did ultimately go wrong, if he did turn out to be just another user, the result would be devastating.

Time seemed to lose its meaning on the trail. The days melded together, measured not by the clock but by Beth and Brian's progress. They trekked the high ridges along the spine of the Appalachians, their rugged northerly course marked by all the evidences of spring—the new green of the chinquapins, the drifts of white trillium, the songs of the Carolina wren.

Beth enjoyed all of it, or would have if her heart and mind hadn't been so torn over the man hiking beside her. To his credit, Brian kept his promise. There was never another provocative word or action out of him. What that cost him she would never know. His careful restraint should have helped her state of indecision. It didn't when his presence alone was seduction enough. Complicating the whole problem was the growing ease and naturalness of their togetherness on the trail, the uncanny ability he had of anticipating her moods, the fun he made out of even a mundane necessity like washing their clothes in a village launderette. Damn it, how was she supposed to make up her mind about him when he was such a great companion?

The week was marred by only one disturbing occurrence. They were stopping overnight at a family campground in Great Smoky Mountains National Park. Taking advantage of the facilities there that the regular shelter sites seldom offered, Beth was just coming away from one of the shower stalls when a pair of giggling teenage girls approached her.

The less shy of the two thrust a paper and pencil under her nose. "Would you give us your autograph, Ms. Holland?"

Beth was amused. "My autograph? Now why would you possibly want *my* autograph?"

"Well, you are a celebrity, aren't you?"

"Celeb— Where did you ever get that idea? Wait a minute. How do you know my name?"

"We watched you go into the shower, and we recognized you. See?" She held up a North Carolina newspaper. Beth's photo and the story of her hike stared back at her.

My God, she thought, alarmed, what kind of publicity campaign has Annie cranked up on me? An extensive one, obviously, if kids were starting to ask for her autograph.

Beth was even more worried when she borrowed the paper and read the article. Apparently, she and Brian had become something of a hot issue. The paper was referring to the hike as a conflict between the Yankee naturalist and the Reb builder, a contest made more alluring to the public by the suggestive fact that the two of them were alone together on the trail.

She was going to kill Annie! This was exactly the sort of attention she didn't want, an honest cause degenerating into some gleeful media sideshow with legions following their progress and taking sides over them. Besides, the whole thing was getting downright scary. The environmental community was not only watching her, they were counting on her. What if she let them down?

Beth wasted no time in finding a phone and calling Atlanta.

"Now, Beth," Annie soothed her after she had wailed her objections, "I didn't suggest anything at all lurid like that in my releases. I just gave them the facts, and they took it from there. I'll try to put a control on it, but I don't want you worrying about it."

"But my bosses—"

"The Green Guards are thrilled with the publicity, Beth. I've been in touch with them, and they see this as a chance to focus attention on an important matter. They've even got hiking clubs around the country helping to get the word out. They're behind you all the way, so just relax and hang in there. Gotta go now. I have a client on the other phone."

Beth was less reassured than Annie wanted her to be when she came away from the phone. She thought immediately of Brian. There was no way she could keep this publicity buildup from him, nor did she want to. She was finding that she had the urge to be open with him, to share everything.

And that, too, was scary...but somehow wonderful at the same time.

Beth showed him the story over supper that evening and was relieved when he didn't seem particularly concerned by it. "Your friend is right," he advised her gently. "Forget about all the hoopla and concentrate on the trail. That's what matters, isn't it?"

He's thinking about me, she realized with a glow of pleasure. Not about himself or Hobart, but about me.

She crawled into her sleeping bag that night with the conviction that Annie was entirely wrong about Brian McArdle. Being Hobart's man didn't make him a villain. He was much too principled for that. Hadn't he proved that all this week?

Time for a decision about him, Beth. What's it going to be?

But there was no contest. She had already made up her mind to trust him. In the morning she was going to let him know that, and if nature wanted afterward to take its course she'd let it.

She never got the chance to tell Brian. The sun was just peeking through the beeches when she was awakened by a hand rocking her sleeping bag. Startled, Beth opened her eyes to see one of the uniformed park rangers bending over her.

"Ms. Holland?" the young woman whispered, careful not to wake Brian, who was sleeping nearby.

"Yes."

"There's a phone call for you down in the office. The party says it's very important. Can you come?"

Five

Beth's hand was shaking as she reached for the phone waiting for her on the office counter. It had to be Annie. No one else knew she was at this particular campground. But she had talked to Annie yesterday. What could be so serious that her friend was already calling her back?

Her voice was strained as she addressed the mouthpiece. "Annie, is that you?"

Annie could discern the worry in her tone and was quick to relieve her anxiety. "Yeah, it's me again. Don't get scared. It's not an emergency, but they won't call campers to the phone unless it's urgent. Well, I didn't exactly lie. It's important, at least important enough that I had to catch you before you headed out again."

"All right, Annie, what is it?"

There was a brief silence, and then her friend's suspicious "Is your trail buddy there with you?"

"Brian? No, he's still in his sleeping bag."

"That's what I hoped for when I picked another ungodly hour to call you. Otherwise, I would have tried phoning last night, but I was afraid he might be standing right beside you. I mean, I've been getting the impression you two have gotten pretty close. Beth, I'm asking you again: you haven't gone and fallen for him already, have you? Please tell me you haven't fallen for this guy."

"Annie, what's this all about? Another wild Brian McArdle mystery? Because if you've called with a new warning—"

"Beth, it's not just rumor this time, or speculation either. It's—fact."

Annie's voice was suddenly unfamiliar. The tone was definitely subdued, even grave. Her friend had told her not to be frightened, but how could she not be when Annie rarely sounded serious, even when she was serious? She fought the tremor in her own voice. "I guess you'd better let me have it then."

"Beth, I'm sorry. I have the worst feeling this is going to matter, and I'm really sorry."

"Annie, get to the point, please."

"Your Brian McArdle—he doesn't just represent the Hobart Development Company, Beth. He *is* the company. Well, half of it, anyway."

There was a distinct sinking sensation somewhere in the area under her ribs that she combated with immediate disbelief. "That's crazy! It's just not possible! Charles Hobart owns the Hobart Development Company!"

"*Half* of it," Annie stressed. "It's a family affair. I think their mother also benefits in some way."

"What are you saying? That Brian and Charles are half brothers?"

"You got it."

"Annie, that can't be right!"

"It is right," her friend insisted. "It was in one of the news pieces that came back to me yesterday, and after I read it I checked around. It's true."

"There has to be a mix-up. He wouldn't be out on the trail with me all this time if he was a Hobart owner. He couldn't afford to be gone from the company that long."

"He could if it was important enough to his company, and apparently it is. Beth, face it, he lied to you."

Beth found she was no longer standing beside the counter. She was leaning against it weakly. She was dealing with shock, but under the shock she suddenly recognized the truth. And the bitter disappointment. Brian had told her he was a troubleshooter for Hobart, giving the impression he was simply another member of their construction force. From the beginning she had felt that his explanation was too vague. Obviously, her instinct had been correct, but her emotions had denied it. And now...

She straightened at the counter, facing the situation. "Annie, why didn't we know all this before? I mean, it's such an obvious thing, how could we not have known it?"

She could picture her friend shrugging. "It's a dumb slipup, I know, but it happens. I suppose the people who were aware of his ownership simply assumed we had to be aware of his ownership, too. So it somehow never got mentioned or picked up in any of the stories, either, until now. Also, he handles the field end of the business, so he's not in Atlanta much. One of my sources tells me he prefers to keep in the background and let his brother take care of the up-front stuff. And don't forget, the company is called Hobart after his stepfather, who started it. Beth?"

"Yes?"

"What are you going to do about him?"

"I—I don't know. I'll have to think about it."

"Beth, you can't let this make a difference. You have to go on."

"Don't worry," she promised Annie with a grim edge to her voice. "I'll go on, all right. That's a definite. The only question now is whether I go on alone after I've finished with Hobart's co-owner."

It struck her as she was coming away from the park office that, for the first time since she could remember, Annie hadn't been dealing with some household crisis while she talked on the phone. Instead, Beth was dealing with a crisis of her own.

Just how bad is it? she wondered as she made her way back to their campsite. Bad enough, she decided, remembering that she had been on the point of trusting him completely. That made his betrayal hurt all the more. And when she thought of his passion the night he had cut her hair, and her own treacherous response to his kiss, her hurt deepened. By the time she regained the campsite she was heartsick and angry, but able to temper both emotions with one small consolation. The situation could have been worse, much worse, had she permitted an involvement beyond that kiss. Or was it already too late? No! She refused even to consider that.

Brian had their sleeping bags secured to the packs and breakfast waiting when she joined him. "Starting to get a little worried here about you, Yank. Where did you get to?"

"Just down the hill." She wasn't ready to offer a better explanation. Of course, she was going to confront him about this latest disclosure. There was no question of that, and this time she meant to have the full truth without any game-playing on either side. But not just yet. She wanted to choose the right moment for the confrontation, and somehow this wasn't it. She needed to think first, to be sure of her words when she faced him.

Brian offered no further question about her absence, but she caught him watching her thoughtfully as they downed a hasty breakfast and began to prepare their packs. Trust him to be vigilant with every little thing, she thought sourly. But then I guess you don't get to be the owner of your own company without being vigilant. Yes, and since he had withheld that little fact from her, then all the rest was probably true as well. Undoubtedly, he *was* out here to sabotage her hike, and employing whatever low methods he could.

"We're awfully quiet this morning," Brian finally observed.

It's called being in a black mood, McArdle, and you're responsible for it, she thought. Better lighten up, though, before this ends up with that scene you're not ready for.

"Sorry," she apologized. "I guess it's the weather. What happened to our sun?"

He straightened up from his packing, considering the now overcast sky. "It's spring in the South, Beth, and that means rain. We've just been lucky so far, but could be we've had it."

"Then I guess we'd better head out now and make time while we can."

It was a miserable morning. They weren't twenty minutes on the trail before a cheerless drizzle began to fall, the kind of gray wetness that promises to persist throughout the day. The terrain was not good, either. There was a lot of rough ascending and descending of muddy, tricky slopes, the trail so narrow and rocky in this wild section that it had to be negotiated single file.

There wasn't the opportunity to talk much, and Beth was glad for that. Although the heavy going made a ready excuse for their silence, she was afraid Brian was sensing the strain between them. His habitual humor wasn't there, and she reproached herself for missing it so much.

In fact, there was a lot she minded as she trudged up the path behind him, hunched inside her all-weather poncho, which seemed to collect as much rain as it shed. Brian swung along in front of her, the sight of his tall, brawny figure dismaying her. How could she still find that body so sexy after what she had learned this morning?

And you thought all those muscles came from heavy construction work, she chided herself. They're probably the result of expensive health club equipment. And when are you going to face him down? What are you waiting for, coward?

Early in the afternoon the weather worsened, the steady drizzle of the morning thickening into penetrating sheets of rain. Five minutes into the downpour, Brian turned to her with a brusque "This is nuts! I'm tired and wet, you're tired and wet, and nothing says we have to go on walking in this crummy stuff!"

Beth faced him stubbornly. "Hikers don't make it to Maine if they hole up somewhere every time the weather turns a little bad. I've walked in worse. What's the matter? Aren't you tough enough?"

He gazed down at her, craggy jaw tightening over her defiant challenge. "And they don't make it to Maine if they land in a hospital somewhere with pneumonia."

Beth sighed. He had a point, and there was no sense in letting her angry heart rule her head. "All right, I guess we should stop until it lets up a bit, but just where do you suggest we take cover? The next shelter is miles ahead."

"There." He pointed to a cliff rising from the forest just off to the left of the path. "Looks like a pretty good overhang to me."

She nodded and followed him through the dripping trees and across the slick rocks. The cliff provided better than an overhang. Nature had hollowed out a high, shallow stone grotto, dry and snug except for a trickle of water that fed a little pool rimmed by moss and ferns. In any other circumstances, Beth would have considered it a charmed spot, but in her present mood . . .

Brian jerked his head in the direction of a stack of boulders. "That should be private enough for you to climb out of those wet things."

"Since when are you giving the orders?" she grumbled, but she complied and went behind the rocks to change into a dry outfit.

She returned to find Brian perched on a moss-cushioned ledge inside the entrance to the grotto. He had changed his own wet clothing for dry jeans and a sweatshirt. His pack was slung down beside him. He moved it aside and patted the place next to him, indicating she should join him.

Beth hesitated, but since it was the only flat place to settle, she sank beside him. They stared out in silence at the curtains of rain. Or rather, she gazed at the rain. He had turned his head, and she could feel those blue-green eyes searching her. Damn it, why did every little thing about him have to look so good?

She heard him clearing his throat, and she thought, here it comes.

"I'd like to think," he said, his voice even deeper than usual, "that this grumpy mood of yours is just a result of the weather, but something tells me it's not. All right, Beth, let's have it. What happened at the campground this morning?"

She didn't answer him. She went on watching the rain.

"Come on," he insisted, "it's time to clear the air here."

She knew he was right. She should have faced him with Annie's revelation the moment she had rejoined him at their campsite. Instead, she had made excuses to postpone her accusation. Why? *Be honest now, Beth.* Maybe because, despite the facts, she had wanted to preserve her wonderful illusions about him just a little longer. But no more delays. She decided to get it over with and give him what he was asking for.

She turned to him, her voice cold. "There was a phone call for me at the park office. It was from my friend in Atlanta. She had a piece of interesting news to share." She went on to tell him what Annie had learned.

When she was finished, Brian surprised her with the mildness of his reaction. He nodded, his voice calm. "I thought it must be something like that. I didn't expect to keep it from you forever."

Her own expression was frigid. "Just long enough to defeat my hike, I suppose."

The deep eyes probed hers. "Is that what you think, Beth? That I'm using you for my own gain, just like those other guys you told me about?"

"What else am I supposed to think? You lied to me about your connection with Hobart, didn't you?"

He shook his head vigorously. "I never lied to you about what I am, not once. I am a kind of on-the-job troubleshooter for the outfit. That's what I do, essentially, and it does keep me out in the field for the company."

"Yes, and at the same time you're one of its owners, something you deliberately withheld from me. So, it's all a question of semantics, isn't it? In the end it comes down to one thing: you misrepresented yourself from the start."

His answer was quick and heated, startling her. "Would you have stood for me hiking right beside you if you had known I was half of Hobart?"

Her own reply was equally swift. "Absolutely not."

He smiled wryly. "There's your explanation then."

"That's no explanation at all. It doesn't begin to tell me why the co-owner of a company like Hobart Development is prepared to leave his business to go tramping through the wilderness for weeks on end with someone he's never met, unless—"

"Unless what? He's out to ruin you somehow? That's called 'jumping to conclusions,' Beth."

"Then why did you come with me when someone far less valuable than the head of the company could have monitored my hike for you?"

His body, which had been as rigid as hers, slumped tiredly. "Look, it didn't start out that way. Charlie had made a mess of things, and I came up to that motel to, well, frankly, to check you out. I had to learn for myself just what Hobart was up against, didn't I? When a business has something important in the works, as Hobart does with this project in Maine, then it's only smart to know exactly who or what might be threatening that venture—something my brother should have remembered before he went out on that limb with you."

"Are you telling me that you never intended to accompany me at all?"

"Not the whole distance, no. Only far enough to see just how genuine you were and whether you were capable enough to actually make Maine. And that's *all* I ever meant to do."

"Then why have you come all this way with me?" she demanded. "You must have been able to tell by the end of the first day what kind of endurance and determination I had."

"Because from the minute you opened that motel room door and I saw you, there was no way I was going to let you walk off to Maine all on your own. I convinced Charlie it was in our best interests for me to tag along." His gaze sought hers, as penetrating as a lover's. "Oh, hell, Beth, how much plainer can I make it? I wanted to be with you, and it seemed the only way. Do you see?"

He leaned toward her, and his sensual nearness was as tempting as ever, but her mistrust was too deep this time to permit another easy surrender. She edged away from him on the rock.

"And just when were you planning to tell me that you're half of Hobart?"

"When it seemed safe enough. When I'd convinced you to stop being suspicious of me at every turn in the path. Damn it, Beth, I was scared. You had this history of men letting you down. I was afraid that if you knew the truth before you completely trusted me, you'd think the worst, and that's just what is happening, isn't it?" He grunted softly in frustration. "Let me tell you something, lady! I've gone through misery this week keeping my hands off you because that's the way you wanted it! You think I would have exercised that kind of restraint unless it did matter what you thought of me?"

She watched him warily. He was sliding toward her along the rock, and before she could stop him, his big hand reached down and caught one of her hands out of her lap.

"No, not this time!" She snatched her hand away.

He swore under his breath and insistently pulled the hand back into his own, long fingers curling tightly around hers, squeezing possessively. "Stop jumping away. I'm not going to pounce on you. All I'm asking for is your hand. Don't deny me this contact, Beth. I need it to try to make you understand. I promise it won't go any further than that. I just want to hold on to you. All right?"

She nodded weakly, willing to give him this much, even though it might be another mistake. But didn't he realize what something even so simple as his hand clinging to hers did to her? "What—what do you want me to understand?"

"About us and where we stand with each other. Beth, I don't want to hide anything from you anymore. I want it all out in the open, so just listen, will you?"

"Go on."

"There's this thing between Charlie and me. It's—well, maybe it's because I'm not just the older brother but the half brother as well. Anyway, he's always had this bit of a jealousy where I'm concerned."

Remembering the dry, solemn Charles Hobart and comparing him now to his charismatic half brother, Beth could well understand that. "What's that got to do with all of this?"

"I'm coming to that. You see, Charlie looks perfectly competent and efficient, and most of the time he actually is. The company runs smoothly, and we get along just fine. But every now and again, usually when I'm out in the field somewhere, this damn rivalry has him trying to get one up on me. That's essentially what happened the day you marched into his office. When you made that offer about hiking the A.T., he saw it as a chance to grab free publicity for Hobart, and he would get the credit. He never seriously believed you could make it to Maine, so he figured the company wouldn't lose anything. Then the story came out in the Atlanta paper the next day about your experience with backpacking and how even grandmothers had walked the A.T. from Georgia to Maine. That's when he realized what a reckless error in judgment he had made and that he might have put the Maine project in jeopardy."

SILHOUETTE.

♥ PRESENTS ♥

A
Real Sweetheart
of a Deal!

**PEEL BACK THIS CARD AND SEE
WHAT YOU CAN GET! THEN...**

Complete the Hand Inside

It's easy! To play your cards right,
just match this card
with the cards inside.
Turn over for more details...

Incredible, isn't it? Deal yourself in <u>right now</u> and get 6 fabulous gifts
ABSOLUTELY FREE.

1. 4 BRAND NEW SILHOUETTE DESIRE® NOVELS—FREE!

Sit back and enjoy the excitement, romance and thrills of four fantastic novels. You'll receive them as part of this winning streak!

2. A LOVELY GOLD-PLATED CHAIN—

FREE! You'll love your elegant 20k gold electro-plated chain! The necklace is finely crafted with 160 double-soldered links and it's electroplate finished in genuine 20k gold. And it's yours free as added thanks for giving our Reader Service a try!

3. AN EXCITING MYSTERY BONUS—FREE!

And still your luck holds! You'll also receive a special mystery bonus. You'll be thrilled with this surprise gift. It is useful as well as practical.

PLUS

THERE'S MORE. THE DECK IS STACKED IN YOUR FAVOUR. HERE ARE THREE MORE WINNING POINTS. YOU'LL ALSO RECEIVE:

4. CONVENIENT HOME DELIVERY

Imagine how you'll enjoy having the chance to preview the romantic adventures of our Silhouette heroines in the convenience of your own home! Here's how it works. Every month we'll deliver 6 new Silhouette Desire® novels right to your door. There's no obligation to buy, and if you decide to keep them, they'll be yours for only $2.24* each! That's a saving of 26¢ per book—plus only 69¢ for postage and handling for the entire shipment!

5. A MONTHLY NEWSLETTER—FREE!

It's our special *"Silhouette" Newsletter* your privileged look at upcoming books and profiles of our most popular authors.

6. MORE GIFTS FROM TIME TO TIME—FREE!

It's easy to see why you have the winning hand. In addition to all the other special deals available only to our home subscribers, when you join the Silhouette Reader Service™, you can look forward to additional free gifts throughout the year.

SO DEAL YOURSELF IN – YOU CAN'T HELP BUT WIN!

You'll Fall In Love With This Sweetheart Deal From Silhouette!

SILHOUETTE READER SERVICE™
FREE OFFER CARD

PLACE YOUR WINNING CARD HERE!

4 FREE BOOKS • FREE GOLD-PLATED CHAIN • FREE MYSTERY BONUS • CONVENIENT HOME DELIVERY • INSIDER'S NEWSLETTER • MORE SURPRISE GIFTS

YES! Deal me in. Please send me four free Silhouette Desire® novels, the gold-plated chain and my free mystery bonus as explained on the opposite page. If I'm not fully satisfied I can cancel at any time but if I choose to continue in the Reader Service I'll pay the low members-only price each month.

326 CIS 816U
(C-SIL-D-06/90)

First Name		Last Name	
PLEASE PRINT			

Address			Apt.

City	Prov.	Postal Code	

Offer limited to one per household and not valid to current Silhouette Desire® subscribers. Orders subject to approval.

SILHOUETTE® NO RISK GUARANTEE

- There is no obligation to buy – the free books and gifts remain yours to keep.
- You'll receive books before they're available in stores.
- You may end your subscription at any time—by sending us a note or a shipping statement marked "cancel" or by returning any shipment to us at our cost.

Remember! To win this hand, all you have to do is place your sticker inside and DETACH AND MAIL THE CARD BELOW. You'll get four free books, a free gold-plated chain and a mystery bonus.

BUT DON'T DELAY!
MAIL US YOUR LUCKY CARD TODAY!

If card is missing write to:
Silhouette Reader Service, P.O. Box 609, Fort Erie, Ontario L2A 5X3

Business Reply Mail

No Postage Stamp Necessary if Mailed in Canada

Postage will be paid by

SILHOUETTE READER SERVICE ™

P.O. Box 609

Fort Erie, Ontario

L2A 9Z9

Canada Post
Postes Canada
125

Beth had trouble concentrating on Brian's story. Now that she was not struggling to withdraw her hand, his lean fingers had relaxed on hers, but they weren't still. They were busy moving over her fingers, slowly stroking them. He was fondling her. It wasn't any deliberate seduction, she was fairly sure of that, but an unconscious caressing.

Beth managed to keep her voice even. "And that's when you came into the picture."

Brian nodded. "Charlie panicked and called me at the downstate project. I told him straight off that I wasn't about to do his dirty work for him and try to back us out of the promise to you. But the situation was serious enough that I agreed to come up and look you over, maybe walk with you a day or two to see that you didn't get into the kind of trouble that would make Hobart look irresponsible. When I met you, I could see right away that you were a fighter and would stick to it and that there was every chance we could lose the right-of-way on the Maine property."

Beth pulled her hand slowly away from his. She had to have a clear head for this, and his absent playing with her fingers was destroying her reason. "Brian, it's just a corridor through the project. Does it matter so much if you lose that to the A.T.?"

He bobbed his head soberly. "It could, yes. It could put the whole development at risk if a public trail runs smack through those luxury units with potential buyers valuing their privacy. Beth, it's not just me or Charles I'm thinking about. To be honest with you, Hobart's funds are strained right now because of this first out-of-state expansion. That means other people are involved, a lot of jobs at stake, and if that project is endangered—"

"But the Appalachian Trail affects people, too!" she cried. "Thousands of people!"

"I know that," he agreed sadly. "Beth, we're not irresponsible land-grabbers. We're going to preserve everything we can in its natural state, but if the A.T. right-of-way on that property isn't relocated..." He didn't finish. The rest was obvious.

"And where does all that put you and me?"

"I don't know, sweetheart," he said softly, his gaze holding hers so closely that she felt her heart turning over. "All I know is that something started to happen between us when you opened that motel room door, and you know it, too."

"Yes," she confessed in a small voice, "I'm afraid I do."

He grinned slowly, his characteristic humor restored. "Damn right. And we're going to find out just how big that something is, because it matters, Beth. It matters a lot."

"Yes, but if—"

"Shh." He laid the tip of a finger against her mouth. "Let it rest, sweetheart. We'll handle it as it comes, but for now..." He inhaled deeply. "Rest. That's exactly what I want to do."

She couldn't help the smile that tugged at the corners of her mouth. "And just where do you plan to bed down?"

"Right here." And with that, he promptly stretched himself along the surface of the mossy rock, hogging most of the space. Without asking, he pillowed his head in her lap. "Ah, better than goose feathers."

"Comfy?" she asked sarcastically, but secretly she was pleased that he had appropriated her lap as though it were his right to do so.

"Mmmm. Wake me when the rain lets up."

Arms folded across his chest, he shut his eyes, relaxed and was instantly asleep.

Beth, resisting the longing to reach down and gently stroke the tousled brown hair away from his forehead where it was pasted in rain-dampened strands, gazed at his solid length, admiring the fit of his faded jeans over muscled thighs, the breadth of his shoulders in the sweatshirt, and knew that she believed him. She had been too moved by the words and actions of his explanation, and the just plain essence of the man he was, not to trust all he had told her. And if he let her down, if her belief now cost her in pain later on...

Later on? Could there even be any later on? Brian was so confident that whatever was between them, whatever they had started to mean to each other, could be resolved that he had been able to simply close his eyes and go to sleep. And she was in turmoil.

How could it work out when the situation was so plainly impossible? She couldn't abandon her hike for him without sacrificing her basic principles or letting the whole environmental community down. All of those supporters were watching and counting on her. And Brian couldn't afford to simply hand over that right-of-way without risking his vital project, which meant that there was no solution to the conflict that stood between them. Whoever won that right-of-way, one of them must lose. She hated this!

Unable to stand the indecision tearing at her, the ache of looking down at that strong, sleeping face pillowed so warmly in her lap, Beth looked up and watched the rain slanting through the trees. For a long time she watched the falling rain while Brian napped, but nothing altered the fact that he stood on one side of a solid barrier and she stood on the other. That was why she came to the conclusion that she did.

She didn't realize she was carelessly shedding tears until Brian blinked open one eye, wiping at a dab of moisture that had dripped on his chin. "Hey, are we getting the rain in here?"

Beth shook her head and turned her face, but he had already noticed her eyes. He swung to a sitting position, his voice hoarse with emotion. "You're crying!" he realized. He started to reach for her, but she held him away.

"It's all right." She wiped at her eyes and faced him. "I'm just being stupid about a practical decision."

"What decision?" he demanded.

"The one I made while you were napping. It's—it's no good our walking on together, Brian. It's not helping either of us except to make us frustrated and unhappy. You know that there's no answer to this whole thing, not one that will work for both of us, and so I think . . . well, I think that before it's too late and we get ourselves hopelessly involved, we should part here and now." Her words quickened, spilling over one another in her haste to get them out before she could change her mind. "Look, you've got your work back there, and you can't go on ignoring it. I mean, they must need you. And it's perfectly safe for me to go on alone. It really is. Haven't I proved that? So anyway, I think that's what we have to do. You'll go back home, and I'll go on with the hike, and maybe down the road, somehow . . ."

She couldn't go on. The look on his face frightened her. The small scar over his left eyebrow, scarcely noticeable ordinarily, had turned very white and very pronounced, like a lightning bolt, and the blue-green eyes were positively stormy.

"Brian?" she asked in a small voice.

And that was when she learned that Brian McArdle was capable of an awesome temper. The ferocity of his reaction to her intention stunned her. In one second he was staring at her in a hot silence. In the next second his powerful hands were gripping her upper arms, his husky voice lashing her.

"The hell you will! Are you listening to me!" he roared. "You'd better be listening to me!"

She was so overwhelmed by his assault that all she could manage to do was mutter a dazed and obedient, "Yes."

"When you walk out of here, I'm going to be walking with you! Same as always! You got that?"

"Y-yes."

"Good, because it's time you understood and accepted the fact that we definitely mean something to each other! How much we mean I don't know, but I intend to find out, and we can't do that if we're apart! Clear?"

"Yes."

"So your hike counts and the project in Maine counts, but maybe we matter as much! And if we do, then we work out all the differences! I don't know how! But I sure as hell do know that the only hope of managing that is by sticking together! You hear me?"

"Yes."

"So that's how we give ourselves a chance! *Together!* Now say yes again."

She gulped, whispering another quick, "Yes."

His hard gaze searched her face, needing to be satisfied that his decision wasn't going to be opposed. That was when he realized she was trembling, and the anger drained out of him instantly. "Lord, I've gone and scared you."

Beth didn't tell him that she was more relieved than frightened, that she was actually thrilled he had taken charge and, with no tolerance for nonsense and a decisive strength, had firmly settled the whole business for them. She let him think she was still alarmed and needed his comforting when, with a small groan, his arms changed direction, slid around her waist and drew her against the hard wall of his chest.

His kiss was in startling contrast to his recent anger and not at all like that desperate kiss the night he had cut her hair. There was nothing hurried and urgent about this kiss. It was patient and tender and agonizingly slow as the tip of his tongue traced the contours of her lips with a sensitive care. Her mouth parted under his, permitting the deep, sweet entry of his tongue. He probed the cavern of her mouth, tasting her, coaxing her to taste him back until their tongues were performing an intimate mating ritual.

The molten fusion of their mouths produced a wild churning in Brian's midsection. His hands shifted on her ribs until they were riding under her breasts, supporting their lush fullness. His thumbs lifted to graze against the peaks. He could feel their reaction, an instant hardening of her nipples and an answering swelling in his groin that fired a primitive urge to wrap his compact body fiercely around hers and bury himself deep inside her. At the same time, as he held her close, experiencing her perfect smallness in contrast to his bigness, the delicate scent of her skin and hair filling his nostrils, he knew a conflicting emotion—the longing to protect her. It amazed him, this enormous feeling of protectiveness. He had never felt so forceful a need with any other woman.

And just because of that need, reason told Brian that this was neither the time nor the place to make the kind of love to her that his arousal demanded. That would have to wait.

But not for long, he promised himself in silent, shuddering frustration as, with a last feathering of kisses along her throat, he reluctantly released her. Not for damn long.

Beth didn't know whether to be relieved or disappointed when Brian held her away. One thing was for sure. Soft or hard, his kisses packed a wallop. No, there was one other certainty: he wasn't going to let her get away. He was going on with her, and all wisdom aside, she had neither the will nor the desire to offer a single further objection. She wanted him right where he had informed her he intended to be, beside her.

"Rain's let up," he said.

"Yes."

"You okay now?"

"Fine."

"We'd better move on then. This is probably only a lull, and we should try to make that next shelter before it starts in again."

They were back to the ordinary business of the hike. Just like that. No, not just like that, either, she realized as they struggled into their packs and returned to the trail. She was exhilaratingly aware of a new intimacy between them now, and she could feel that Brian was aware of it, too.

Trouble was waiting for them less than a quarter of a mile before they reached the shelter. At the bottom of a long hill they arrived on the banks of what was supposed to be a placid creek. But the heavy rains had swollen the stream, drowning the crossing stones under a rushing torrent of water.

Beth considered the situation. "What do you think?"

"What I think is that since there's no bridge and since that sky is looking mean again and since I don't plan to sleep on this side tonight, we'd better try fording it. You wait here and let me cross first."

She didn't argue with his wisdom. He had the long legs for testing the depth and the physical strength for withstanding a current that might prove treacherous for her.

She watched him, pant legs rolled up to his thighs and shoes in hand, feel his way cautiously across the stream. The water never reached above his knees.

"No raging Niagara," he reported from the other side, "but tricky to balance in that current. Maybe I'd better come back and lend you a hand, or we could rig up a line for you to hang on to."

Beth already had her own pant legs rolled up and her shoes hanging by their laces around her neck. She waved him off impatiently. "Don't be silly. I'm coming over. Stay right there."

"Beth, wait, I don't think—"

But she was already plunging into the creek and wading toward him.

She would have been all right, even with the water over her knees, if the sky hadn't decided to open up again as she was halfway across. The downpour was so sudden and heavy, with the lashing rain blurring her vision, that Beth quickened her struggle to reach the opposite bank. This was a mistake. In her careless rush, she caught her foot against one of the submerged stepping-stones, lost her balance and went down like a rock.

The mountain waters had been cold on her legs, but now they were above her waist, and she gasped with the icy shock. She tried to regain her footing, but the tumbling current seemed to be pinning her down. She could feel herself being dragged away from the shallows toward the deeper waters. It was a dangerous predicament, and her helplessness frightened her.

Beth was at the point of being swept downstream when a pair of strong arms closed around her, lifted her and hauled her to safety on the grassy bank.

"Are you all right?" Brian asked, his face thrust close to hers as he frowned with concern.

Beth, huddled on the ground beside him, managed to catch her breath. "I don't seem to have much luck crossing streams, do I? Yes, I'm all here. Even my shoes didn't get away."

"Much good they're going to do you at the moment, or anything else we're wearing. We're both soaked. Come on, let's get out of this rain and up to that dry shelter."

Beth thought that was a wonderful suggestion, until she got to her feet and started to put weight on her left leg. She winced with the sharp pain.

"What is it?"

"I must have banged my knee on that stone when I went down. Damn!"

Brian was instantly crouching at her feet, his fingers gently probing the knee. "How bad is it? Does it hurt a lot?"

"It's—just a little tender. Probably only bruised. Come on, I'll be all right."

But he had been looking up into her face when he questioned her, and he hadn't missed her grimace at the contact of his hand against her knee. "Yes, you will be but not hobbling up that hill. I'll carry you to the shelter."

"Brian, you can't! Our packs—"

"The hell with our packs! We'll leave them here, and I'll come back for them. You want to make Maine, don't you?"

"Yes."

"Well, you won't if you don't give that knee a rest. Remember Daddy and piggyback rides?"

"That's not very romantic."

"No," he agreed dryly, unfastening their backpacks and placing them under a nearby ledge. "But it's a lot more practical than anything else right now. Come on, climb aboard."

She did and traveled up the long slope clinging to his broad back. It was an experience that might have been interesting if they hadn't both been so wet and uncomfortable.

The unoccupied shelter was a welcome sight. Brian deposited her on a bench inside, went back for their packs and returned to find Beth trying not to noticeably shiver.

"This is no good," he announced decisively. "No fireplace in here and no way in this weather to build a fire outside. We're not spending the night here."

"Do we have a choice?"

"Yes. There's a service road out there for the shelter, and roads lead to civilization."

"But that could be miles and—"

"Wait." He had produced the maps and guides and was consulting them. "Here it is. We're in luck. There's a village not far off the service road."

"We can walk to it?"

"Correction: *I* can walk to it where I beg, borrow or steal a vehicle to drive back up here for you. You're staying off that knee."

"Then what?"

"Then we find a motel, rooming house or whatever, and maybe we even get the knee looked at. How is it?"

She was touched by his compassion. "Okay. It's not even swelling much, so that's a good sign."

"You rest it. I'll be back as soon as I can. The rain's stopped again and there's plenty of daylight left so I shouldn't be too long."

He was halfway across the clearing when Beth, hopping to the shelter entrance, stopped him. "Wait," she called. "If I go and spend time off the trail, I could be violating my agreement with Hobart."

"Beth," he reminded her, "*I'm* Hobart, and I say that a reasonable stopover near the trail doesn't constitute any violation of our agreement. Now get back in there and see if there's anything left in your pack that's dry enough to change into. And stay off that leg!"

Exasperating woman, he thought as he turned and strode off along the service road. She'd sleep out here in the wet and cold with a banged-up knee rather than risk her precious hike. Only it wasn't going to be that way. She was going to spend the night in a warm, dry bed, and if he had his way, bad knee permitting, he was going to be in that bed with her. He was through waiting.

Six

———

Darkness had closed in around the shelter, and Beth was starting to worry about Brian's whereabouts, when headlights and the sound of an engine sliced the blackness of the forest. Relieved, she watched through the screens that formed the open end of the shelter as a heavy-duty pickup truck bumped up the rough track and swung into the clearing.

Brian emerged from the passenger door, and a man joined him from the other side. At least Beth thought the burly figure in lumber jacket and Stetson was a man, until the two people stepped into the shelter. Brian was carrying a flashlight, and he introduced his driver.

"Beth, this is Rita, and she's here to rescue you. Say thank you."

Beth grinned at the older woman from her bench. "Thank you, Rita, and bless you."

Rita was of the bluff, no-nonsense variety, and she took charge immediately. "Let's have a look at this knee of yours."

While Brian directed the flashlight, she hunkered down beside the bench, asking Beth how the knee felt. "Better since I've been resting it," Beth assured her.

Callused fingers carefully tested the joint, and she was asked a couple of blunt questions in a resonant voice that she was convinced could boom from one mountain peak to the next if necessary.

Rita, satisfied, got to her feet. "She'll do. Don't think it's anything like torn ligaments or a break. Just a painful contusion."

Beth was perplexed. "Are you a doctor or something?"

Rita laughed. "Honey, in these mountains y'gotta be a bit of everything. Don't worry, if that knee isn't all recovered by tomorrow we'll get you to a real doc over in Honersville, but I think all you need is the ice pack I got waitin' in the truck and a spot of my special liniment back at the house."

Beth relaxed. She had been half-afraid that the knee might end her hike.

"Ready to get down off this mountain?" Brian asked.

She assured him she was, and Rita went off with their backpacks, while Brian, supporting Beth, helped her out to the truck. "Who is she, and exactly where are we going?" Beth whispered to him.

"She's the luck of the Irish," he whispered back. "Right smack where the service road joins the hard road in the valley is Rita's farm. Rita not only raises quarter horses, she also operates a tidy bed and breakfast, and we're booked in for the night. Good?"

"I'm not arguing."

He lifted her into the truck and squeezed in beside her. Reaching for a blanket on the back seat, he started to wrap it around her.

"I don't need that," she objected. "I'm not a trauma victim." The blanket bore a distinct doggy odor.

"You said you weren't arguing," he ordered, "so don't. I can feel you're cold."

Beth huddled in the blanket without another protest, grateful for its warmth and the caring bulk of the man beside her. The blanket's odor was explained when a mournful-looking head appeared over the backrest, the wet nose of a hound dog poking into Beth's ear.

"That's Fred," Brian introduced her.

"Hello, Fred," Beth acknowledged the animal who sniffed disdainfully, then retreated.

Rita, who had been at the back of the truck stowing the packs and digging into her ice chest, joined them up front, sliding behind the wheel. "Here's that ice pack," she said, pressing a cold plastic bag into Beth's hand. "You hug it to that knee, hear, and hang on good 'cause it's all switchbacks going down this mountain."

Within minutes, the truck had cleared the forest and was swooping through the open valley. They turned into a well-lighted farmyard, but Beth was surprised when the pickup kept traveling past the spacious and handsome old farmhouse, following a lane that ended near an apple orchard. Here, in a grove of chestnut oaks, stood what looked like a small, pioneer log cabin with a porch stretched across its front.

"The original homestead on the place," Rita indicated. "Was falling to pieces when I got the farm, but I preserved it and added plumbing and lights. Just use it for guest quarters these days. Hope you like it."

Beth liked it a lot when she was helped from the truck and into the cabin. It consisted of a sitting room with a field-stone fireplace, a single bedroom and an adjoining bath. Thick beams, aged to a silvery color like the log walls, crossed the low ceilings, and simple country pieces in mellow old woods made a counterpoint to bright rag rugs laid on the pine board floor.

"I think I've died and gone to heaven," Beth enthused from the rocker where she had been deposited.

Rita was pleased but still dealing with the practical. "Want to come back to the house with me, Brian, I'll get you that liniment. Think I can scout up a spare pair of pj's and a robe for Beth, too. I know hikers, and you won't have those in your pack, and after that dousing not much that's dry, either, so bring all your clothes and we'll run them through the dryer."

Rita and Brian departed, and Beth headed for the bathroom. She hadn't seen a tub since leaving her motel in Georgia, and she intended to treat herself to a real bath. Careful of the knee, she luxuriated in warm, soapy water.

Oversize bath towel wrapped around her, she stepped out into the bedroom to find flannel pajamas and a robe already waiting on the bed. She was reaching for them when it occurred to her: Uh-oh, only one bed in the whole place and no sofa in the other room, either. How do we deal with that?

As it comes, she decided with a shrug.

The pajamas and robe were a couple of sizes too big for her, but she didn't mind. They were warm and dry.

Brian was kneeling on the hearth coaxing a fire when she opened the door to the sitting room. He eyed her apparel with a glint of mischief.

"I know. I'm swimming in them, but who cares? Do I have to submit to that liniment treatment?"

"Later." He got to his feet. "After I get back from shopping."

"You're going shopping?"

"We have to eat, don't we?"

"Oh, right. I am getting hungry."

"And I don't want rations from our packs tonight. I want a real meal. Rita's loaning me the truck to drive into the village. I'll find a phone to check in with Atlanta and then bring back supper for two. Sound okay?"

"Sounds great."

He left, and Beth was settled happily in the rocker toasting her feet in front of the crackling blaze in the fireplace when someone rapped on the door. She went unwillingly to answer it. She found a young man, barely out of his teens, standing on the porch. He was pencil thin, had solemn blue eyes and sported a blond beard.

"Hi. I'm Rick Hansen. Rita sent me down to fill up your firewood box."

"Oh. I guess it is on the low side. Well, come on in."

She limped back to her rocker, and Rick began hauling in split logs from a cart off the porch, stacking them neatly in the antique box beside the fireplace. She was conscious after a moment that on each trip he eyed her shyly. Clearly, there was something on the young man's mind.

Beth smiled at him encouragingly. "What is it, Rick?"

He stood up from the box, dusting his hands. "You're Beth Holland, aren't you? Rita didn't say, but I thought I recognized you." There was actually a note of awe in his low, gentle voice.

Oh, no, Beth thought, remembering the teenagers who had wanted her autograph, not another one.

"Uh—yes," she reluctantly admitted.

"I thought so." He tugged excitedly at the old denim jacket he wore. "Wow! Wait till I tell the others."

"What others?"

"The other through-hikers out there on the trail. I run into some of them from time to time."

"And they know about me?"

"Well, sure. Word gets around on the trail. That's how I found out about you. We all admire you for what you're trying to do, Ms. Holland."

Beth was uneasy with her celebrity. The last thing she wanted was to be labeled some backwoods folk heroine. "Sounds like you're walking the A.T. yourself, Rick."

"Yeah, I am. Only I'm doing it in this broken sort of way on account of I can't afford to do it straight through like you're doing. So I stop when the money runs out and find jobs, like doing chores here for Rita, and she lets me bunk in the barn. People along the trail are pretty good about hiring you."

"How long have you been out here?"

"The A.T.? Since March. See, it's not really important to me that I hike from start to finish and cover every inch of the trail. Sometimes, I even hitch rides around the boring parts. I guess you could say what I'm trying to do is just get in touch with nature, see the land. Except," he added unhappily, "there are certain people back home who don't understand that." He didn't elaborate.

"Where's home, Rick?"

"Columbus, Ohio. Anyway, what I'm doing matters to me, but what you're doing really counts. I mean, saving our environment stands for something."

"I think so. Except I'm only trying to preserve a little piece of it with this hike, you know."

Rick was still there, eagerly discussing ecology, when Brian returned. When Beth introduced the two of them, Rick got pink in the face, muttered an excuse and abruptly left the cabin.

"Did I say something?" Brian wondered.

Beth laughed. "I think he sees you as the villain of the piece. Word gets around on the trail, you know."

"Huh?"

"Never mind. I'll explain later. What did you bring? I'm starved."

He nodded toward a carton and a bottle he had placed on the table inside the door. "Pizza and red wine. Actually, I was thinking of something more exciting, but it seems this is the best the local eatery can produce on a carryout basis."

"I'm not complaining."

"Tell you what I'll do, though," he said, dragging the table and a chair for himself over to the fireplace. "I'll make up for it by treating you to the real thing at this great inn I know of. It's in Harpers Ferry, West Virginia, and since that's close enough to the halfway point on the trail, you can consider it a celebration."

"It's a deal."

"That is, if you make it that far." She wasn't sure whether his warning was playful or serious. Maybe, considering the stakes, it was something of both.

"Watch me," she guaranteed.

He found plates and a pair of glasses in a cupboard. She leaned forward in the rocker as he poured the wine and lifted the lid of the pizza carton. A savory smell wafted toward her. "I figured you for cheese and sausage," he said, seating himself opposite her.

"You figured right." She helped herself to a slice and bit into it hungrily.

They drank the wine and feasted on the pizza, and Beth grew conscious of a shift in the mood. They were quiet, not bantering with each other now, and she suddenly felt shy with him and altogether too aware of being alone with him in the cabin. Which was silly, considering they had been

alone together out on the trail, but somehow their closeness within these snug four walls was different, more pronounced. She kept thinking of that solitary bed in the other
room, and the image of it made her a little breathless.

When the last slice of pizza had been divided and eaten
after the customary urgings of "You have it," and "No, it's
yours," Brian pushed back from the table and rose to his
feet. He lifted his arms and stretched lazily, and Beth
watched the play of his muscles under his knit shirt, the
straining of cords in his forearms and neck. It was as though
she were discovering the total masculinity of his lithe, compact body for the first time. She felt herself actually color-
ing, and she quickly lowered her gaze.

"I think I'll check out that bathtub for myself," he said
casually. "Then we'll see about the liniment for your knee."

Beth strove to be equally casual. "Go ahead."

He placed a fresh log on the fire and left her. She watched
the flames curling around the new log and tried to relax,
willing herself not to think about what this liniment treatment might involve but unable to curb a mounting anticipation that bordered on excitement. This was embarrassing!
she thought. What if he wasn't—

The bedroom door opened, and Brian appeared in the
sitting room. "Decided on a quick shower instead. My hair
needed it."

Beth looked up from her rocker and managed to swallow
a gasp. He had nothing but a towel wrapped around his lean
flanks, and not a very large towel at that. Six feet of raw,
male magnificence confronted her—a tawny body replete
with wide, hard shoulders, slim hips and long, powerful
legs.

He must have noticed the widening of her eyes. "What's
wrong?" he wondered innocently, his fingers absently
scratching the pelt of curling hair on his chest. It was sev-

eral shades darker than the thatch of sun-lightened hair on
his head, which was still damp and appealingly tousled from
his shower. He looked down at the towel. "Oh, this. Sorry,
but Rita didn't offer any pj's or robe for me, and I wasn't
going to climb back into the grubby stuff I was wearing.
She'll have our other things clean and fresh for us in the
morning. You don't mind, do you?"

"No," she choked.

"Good. You ready for the liniment rub?"

"Ac-actually, I don't need it. I mean, there's really nothing wrong with the knee now. It feels just fine."

He wasn't listening to her. He was glancing around the
sitting room. "We'll have to handle it on the bed. No place
for you to stretch out in here."

"It—it seems funny this place doesn't have a sofa. Is it
necessary that I stretch out?"

"Best way for me to get at you."

"Oh."

"Come on. Into the bedroom."

In a slight daze, Beth rose from the rocker and moved toward the bedroom, Brian following with the bottle of liniment and a hand towel. She perched stiffly on the edge of
the bed, in two minds about what was to happen.

"Robe off and pajama leg pushed up," he instructed.

She rose to obey him, then went back to sitting on the
edge of the bed, her feet planted safely on the floor.

"Beth," he said patiently, "you're going to have to
cooperate with this action. Stretched out, remember?"

"Right."

Swinging her legs off the floor and onto the bed, she lay
back against the pillows piled against the brass headboard.
Brian settled near the lower end of the bed. She watched
nervously as he uncapped the bottle and shook liniment into
the palm of his hand. He leaned forward to examine the

knee. "Some discoloration, but otherwise it doesn't look too bad. This will fix you up."

He began gently to apply the liniment, rubbing in slow circles. The contact of his strong hand against her flesh sent tremors up her spine.

"Relax," he commanded. "You're all tense, and that won't help."

He was right. She was being an idiot about this. Say something, Beth, she chided herself. "At least the stuff doesn't smell bad. I was afraid it might. Liniment can, you know. Do you suppose Rita uses it on her quarter horses?" She'd wanted to speak, not babble.

"Mmm, I wouldn't be surprised, but I saw them out in the pasture, and they all look real healthy to me."

He concentrated on the treatment, his fingers stroking soothingly, working in the healing liniment.

"You—you're very good at this," she observed in a small voice. He was better than good. His hand felt wonderful. She could feel herself beginning to drift, control slipping away from her.

"A deep massage technique I learned back in my soccer days. Works wonders on certain injuries."

"Yes," she agreed, suspecting this was no medical treatment but a highly sensual performance made all the more erotic by his near nudity. She could actually feel the animal heat emanating from those expanses of sinewy flesh bending toward her, could smell the pine-scented soap he had used in his shower. Her head sank back into the pillows, eyes closing in mindless euphoria.

His hand stilled, his weight shifting nearer on the bed. She could sense his new closeness, feel his warm breath on her face. Her eyes fluttered open to find his nose almost touching hers, his sultry gaze searching her expression, questioning.

She could read his desire and what he intended to do about it, and she somehow found the courage to whisper, "Was the liniment medication or was it plain seduction?"

"What do you think?" he asked, his voice low and smoky.

She hesitated, then confessed boldly, "I think either way I'm glad." *Don't fight it, Beth. Let it happen.*

Because it *was* going to happen. She could see it in the thick urgency registered in the eyes locked with hers, could hear it in his slow, earthy growl. "Do you have any idea what you've been doing to me all this damned eternal week? How I've fantasized about us?"

"Tell me," she urged, conscious of her own sudden, elemental craving and the need to answer it.

Tell her? he thought. And risk scaring her off this bed before I have the chance to teach her what we both want? She would probably be shocked by the wanton depth of his fantasies. He was almost shocked by them—the fierce, fiery longings to have those shapely legs of hers wrapped around him tightly, that luscious little body with the alluring bottom going all wild under his while he drove into her repeatedly, eliciting her hot cries of passion.

"Why don't I show you instead?" he drawled, his words slurring with mounting ardor.

She didn't resist when his hands traveled under the loose pajama top. God, she was wearing nothing underneath! It was all there for him. He filled his hands with the sweet fullness of her breasts, explored their silky contours and heard her quickening breath. It wasn't enough. His hands emerged, his shaking fingers working at the buttons until he had the top open and pulled aside.

His head lowered, mouth pressed to a milky mound, curling tongue caressing a taut bud as he tasted the lushness of her, enticing mewing little cries of pleasure from her.

It satisfied him when he finally lifted his head and found her eyes all glazed and dewy as she gripped his shoulders. But still not enough. Maybe, with her, nothing would ever be enough. But he wasn't about to stop trying, he decided as he lowered his lips to hers.

There was a roaring in Beth's ears when Brian's mouth captured and devoured hers, the long, slow thrusts of his penetrating tongue simulating the ultimate love act, telling her more plainly than words what he wanted.

Her hands descended from his shoulders and across his chest, fingers burying themselves in an expanse of crisp hair until she found his hard nipples, pinching and rubbing them provocatively while he moaned low in his throat. She loved the solid substance of him, the tensile muscles of his chest and back.

Breaking the kiss, he drew away from her, his voice raspy. "Look at me! Look what you do to me!"

She did look, and the swelling under the towel caught around his waist was proof of his full arousal. Then, suddenly, the towel was no longer there. He had whipped it away, baring his throbbing masculinity. And somehow her pajama top and bottom were also disposed of, and he was stretched beside her in the bed, gathering her nakedness to his nakedness.

Oh, sweet heaven, the feel of him! His mouth and hands all over her! Husky voice crooning words of encouragement! Teeth carefully, tenderly nipping and tugging! Fingers stroking and preparing all her secret places!

"Your knee," he muttered.

"It's nothing! Don't stop!"

Just when and how he clad himself in the protection he must have secured from his wallet on the bedside table Beth had no idea. She was in a drugged state when his inflamed body rose over hers, settling between her parted thighs. His savage command startled her. "Open your eyes, Beth! I want your eyes open when we come together! I want us looking into each other's eyes!"

She obeyed him, her lids fluttering open to find his gaze slamming into hers with a searing intensity.

He was right! Their joining, when it occurred, was all the more consuming because their eyes were uniting as well, expressing to each other a wealth of meaning and feeling as the heat-seeking missile of his manhood sought, found, then filled the core of her womanhood.

He was a formidable lover, his strokes long and deep, surging with power. Straining to him, Beth responded to his ancient rhythms, to his purrings of endearment—those dark and primitive urgings of man to woman during the ultimate intimacy.

As their love dance increased in tempo, his whispers blurred to rumbles that originated deep within his chest, rose to become lusty growls from his throat and climaxed in the last stages of their sweet frenzy to an exultant shout of male release.

Shaken with spasms, Beth shared his abandonment. She was sobbing with ecstasy when the world fragmented into shards of blinding brilliance, sending her over the edge into a roaring oblivion.

For long minutes, savoring the lethargic glow that bathed their clasped, moist bodies, they were unable to stir, lost to a drowsy, contented heaviness. Then Brian raised his head from her shoulder, his slumberous gaze needing to assure him of her well-being. Her eyes were closed, and she was not aware that he was studying her. He saw the face of a woman who has just been loved, her lips red and swollen from his kisses, her cheeks flushed and at peace. The sight moved him, filled him with wonder and a strange tugging in his vitals.

She felt his gaze. Her eyes opened, and she smiled up at him. He grinned down at her, as sheepish as a boy. "I got carried away with the noises," he said apologetically.

"I noticed."

"Sorry, but it was pretty intense stuff for me."

"For me, too, and I liked your noises. Where are you going?" He was lifting himself away from her, and she missed his weight.

"Nowhere," he said as he settled close beside her, hugging her to him. "Did I hurt your knee?"

"The knee is all better. Stop fussing."

"I will."

They lay there, warm and languid.

Another minute passed, and then he said with satisfaction, "Sometimes it's nice to just cuddle. Nothing else, just cuddle. You know?"

"I know."

Elevating himself on one elbow, he mischievously placed the tip of his finger against the small depression in her nose. "What do you know?"

"A lot of things. Like I love it when you hold me this way, and that inside this big tough body—" she nudged him in the ribs "—lurks a softie."

"Yeah? What else?"

Beth frowned, realizing that there was a great deal about him that she didn't know, and she wanted to know everything. "You tell me."

"Like what?"

"I don't know. How about your family for starters? You said you had a wife once. What ever became of her?"

He hesitated, making her wonder if he was unwilling to discuss his ex-wife. She had had that impression once before when the subject came up. He did answer her then, but he seemed a bit clipped about it. "Trudy? She married a businessman after our divorce and is now leading a happy social life in Atlanta."

"Regrets?" She had to ask, didn't she? She was already a little jealous.

He shook his head. "No regrets."

Could his brevity on the subject of his ex-wife mean he still cared for Trudy? No, he said he had no regrets, and she believed him. "I take it you didn't have any kids."

"No time. We weren't married that long."

"So, now there's just your mother and Charles."

"Right." He was perfectly relaxed now as his fingers trailed over her stomach, drawing little patterns around her navel. "As for my father, I don't even remember him. He walked out when I was an infant. My mother had a tough time of it until she married Chuck Hobart. He was a good man, a real father to me. I still miss him."

"That's something we share, Brian. Stepfathers, I mean. I don't remember my own father, either. He died when I was little, and I lost my stepdad just a few months ago. It was hard. Harder on my mother, though. She depended on him a lot. So, you were close to your stepfather, too?"

"Yep. I worked construction with him growing up, learned the business that he left to Charlie and me. Hobart was just a small, local outfit then."

Hobart. There was no escaping the subject, was there? Even in this sweet moment, she must be reminded of the impossible conflict that lay between them.

His fingertips felt the slight stiffening of her body. "What's wrong?"

She didn't want to be haunted by that conflict. Not tonight, at least. She wanted to chase away its shadow. "Nothing. Come on, we're not through here. I want to know lots more."

So Brian, maybe sensing her fear, told her trivial but revealing things about himself, like the junk food he sometimes had a weakness for and the harmonica he had learned to play as a kid and still loved. And Beth told him about her bald eagles at the Wisconsin sanctuary where she worked and that she was a sucker for old movies, especially the ones from the thirties with slinky Jean Harlow types.

After this swapping of likes and dislikes, they made love again—a slow, tender love this time. When they crawled under the covers finally and fell asleep, Brian held her through the night, his big arms and legs wrapped around her, and Beth, contented in his possessiveness, was able to hold back all the threats. For that night, anyway. In the morning, reality was with them again.

Seven

They were having breakfast in the big, old-fashioned dining room of the farmhouse when Rita interrupted them.

"Phone for you, Brian. Atlanta, I think. You can take it back in my office. How's the knee, Beth?"

"Good as new, thank you. The liniment helped."

Brian went off to his call, and Beth continued with her meal, wondering how Atlanta knew he was here. Then she remembered he'd said last night when he went out for the pizza that he was going to check in with his office.

Brian was gone a long time, and when he returned she knew immediately that something was wrong. He looked worried and unhappy. "What is it?"

"Are you finished?"

"Yes."

"Come on outside. I have to talk to you."

She left the table and followed him into the yard. They stood under a fragrant lilac bush, and he took both her hands and held them tightly. "Beth, I have to leave."

She gazed at him fearfully. "What do you mean?"

"I have to go back to Georgia. There's trouble at our downstate project, a labor thing. Charles thought he could handle it when I talked to him last night, but it seems now that he can't. I don't have any other choice. Damn!"

Beth found herself being reasonable about the situation when she felt anything but reasonable. "Well, of course, you don't, not when it's an emergency. Your company is important."

"And *we're* important," he said angrily. "Look, I don't know how long this thing is going to take. It involves the union, so it could mean days, but I am coming back when it's settled."

"Brian, I can't just sit here waiting for you. I have to go on with the hike."

"I realize that, but I certainly don't relish the idea of you being out there on your own."

"I'll be fine," she assured him. "The knee's all recovered, and now that the weather has turned warmer there will be plenty of other hikers on the trail. But are you sure you'll be able to rejoin me?"

"There's no way I won't," he promised grimly.

"How will you know where I'll be?"

"Harpers Ferry, West Virginia, remember? We have a dinner date there at my inn." He released her hands to pull a slip of paper out of his pocket. "I've written down the number where I can be reached at the project. You call me, *regularly*. I want to know where you are and what's happening at all times. The name of the inn is here also. You check into it, and by the time you get there, I should be able to fly back and meet you. I hate this!"

Beth did, too, more than she could bear to let him know, but there was one small advantage in this depressing situation. When he was with her, she was so affected by him that she was unable to think clearly. Apart from him, she would have the opportunity to search her feelings without the intrusion of wild emotions, hopefully to discover exactly what Brian McArdle did mean to her. And maybe he needed this time-out as well to make a few decisions. After all, there had been no mention yet of any commitment between them, permanent or otherwise.

Beth drew a deep, steadying breath. "How are you getting back to Georgia?"

"I've already made all the arrangements. There's an airfield just up the road. I can charter a plane there. Rick's driving me over in the pickup." He dropped her hands and held our his arms. "Come here," he commanded softly. She did, stepping into his arms, which slid around her waist, drawing her close. "I'm going to miss you," he murmured, cheek against her hair. "Like crazy."

"I know. Me, too."

He kissed her then, a long, feverish kiss that conjured up poignant memories of last night's unrestrained lovemaking in the cabin. Their goodbye was interrupted when the truck pulled into the yard.

Rick leaned from the window with a friendly, "I have all your gear collected and on board, Mr. McArdle."

Brian must have worked his people charm again, Beth decided. Rick's resentment of him last night as the enemy seemed to have magically turned into a warm respect.

Brian reluctantly released her, and she already felt empty as his arms left her. Maybe he sensed that, because in a last, moving gesture, his hand reached out and for a second rested lovingly on the cap of her chestnut hair. Then he turned and climbed aboard the truck, calling from the window a grinning, encouraging, "West Virginia, Yank! Count on it!"

Beth watched the truck until it was out of sight. Then she turned and wandered down the lane toward the cabin. The best thing she could do for her forlorn mood was to get back to the trail and try to hike it out of her system.

She had loaded her backpack and was ready to slip into it and depart when the pickup returned and a breathless Rick intercepted her on the porch.

"I hurried so I wouldn't miss you."

She thought he had come to say goodbye. "Did Brian get off all right?"

"They were fueling up a small twin-engine for him when I left. There's something I want to ask you."

"What is it?"

"Would you mind if I went back to the trail with you? It would be a real honor to hike with you, Ms. Holland. That is," he added shyly, "if you wouldn't mind the company."

Beth was surprised. "You can afford to move on?"

"Well, I've saved enough by now. At least to take me as far as the halfway point, and then I'll probably have to find work again."

"But I'm leaving right away, Rick. Won't Rita mind if you suddenly desert her?"

"No, see, she knows I was only temporary and that it was getting time for me to go back to the trail."

Beth considered the prospect. Rick was a pleasant guy, a bit naive maybe in his youth and gentleness, but trustworthy, she felt. She made up her mind. "I'll be glad of your company, Rick."

But she was already lonely for the hiking companion she really wanted.

* * *

As Beth and Rick trekked northward through the spectacular Shenandoah country, spring followed them like a high tide. They were treated to an endless and glorious succession of rioting mountain laurels, mist-clad peaks, sunny river valleys and the music of nesting songbirds.

They met other young hikers on the trail. Rick seemed to know most of them, and when he proudly introduced Beth, they were eager to meet and talk to her. They were a warmhearted lot, sharing their easy camaraderie and impressed with her mission. But their friendly company was no substitute for that of the man she preferred. She sorely missed Brian.

She called him every chance she got, but talking to him on the phone was not the same as experiencing his crazy humor, not to mention his fervent touch. They endeavored to console each other with the promise of Harpers Ferry, but to Beth that seemed an eternity away.

There were other people she called as well. She checked in with her employers, the Green Guards, who were pleased with her progress. She phoned her mother back in Milwaukee, who worried about motherly things, such as whether Beth was eating properly and avoiding poison ivy. Beth assured her she was. And, of course, she kept in touch with Annie.

Annie had another warning for her as she neared Harpers Ferry. "Watch yourself, Beth. Something is definitely up."

"What do you mean?"

"I don't know, but the rumors are flying back here that Hobart has something new in the works about your hike. I see it as trouble, so just stay on your toes, please. If I find out what it is, I'll let you know."

Rumors, Beth thought, hanging up. That's all it is. Brian wouldn't pull something, and he wouldn't let Charles try anything that would endanger the hike. She didn't want to listen to Annie. She was in love.

In love? Yes, she realized in a kind of slow shock, I'm actually in love with Brian. Now, just when did that happen? Or had she been in love with him all along and, until now, had simply never dared put a name to it? And wasn't it curious that she should discover her condition when he was hundreds of miles away? Well, maybe that wasn't so unusual, either. Instinct, if not experience, suggested to her that if you missed someone desperately enough, you were bound to ask yourself exactly why that was. Maybe you'd even come up with the answer. And it looked as if she had. Love, huh?

Beth moaned about it a little. It was the worst kind of love, too—the sort that pained in its intensity, especially when you didn't know whether the recipient shared your feelings. As, in this case, she didn't. But she refused to worry about it. There had been no time for Brian to express his feelings.

Don't rush it, she reminded herself. Give it time. What you have to do now is concentrate on the hike and let the rest take care of itself in Harpers Ferry.

Which was exactly what she did.

The wild strawberries were ripening on the open hillsides, evidence that spring was giving way to summer, when Beth and Rick finally reached Harpers Ferry—a Civil War town nestled at the confluence of the Shenandoah and Potomac Rivers and looking untouched by time.

It wasn't yet noon when they arrived, and as did most hikers, they headed immediately for the old stone building that housed the headquarters of the Appalachian Trail Conference, administrators of the A.T.

Beth was warmly welcomed and lauded for her effort. Reluctant at first, she agreed to grant an interview to a local reporter the next morning at her inn. She parted with Rick at the center. He was eager to collect any mail that might have been forwarded to him and to see about lodging and a job for himself. Beth was just as eager to find Brian's inn, which she shortly did.

The place was housed in a former powder mill right on the river and, with its casual country-style ambience, was every bit as appealing as Brian had promised. Beth checked in and was assigned a charming room with a view of the heights surrounding the town and the river just below.

She had a bath and then ate lunch. Afterward she wondered what she was going to do for the remainder of the long day. She knew from their last phone conversation that Brian was not due in until early evening and that she had to keep busy until then or go out of her mind with the anticipation of their reunion.

Suddenly she had an inspiration. The dining room here was far from formal, but that special dinner they were to share in called for something more dressy than anything she was carrying in her backpack. She'd go out and buy a new outfit and then after tonight mail it back to herself in Wisconsin. She suddenly wanted to look pretty and feminine for Brian, so why not?

She visited a couple of shops before she finally settled on a cream-colored linen skirt and a cotton sweater with a floral design across the front. She was off to another store to hunt for matching shoes when she ran into Rick on the street.

He was looking a bit mournful. Beth thought it was because he hadn't had any luck yet with a job, but that wasn't the reason.

Rick wasn't very articulate, but he managed to explain the problem while tugging at his blond beard. "It's the two letters I had waiting for me from Ohio. One from my girl back there and one from my folks. They can't see my being out here. They think I'm being irresponsible, like I was some throwback to the hippie sixties or something."

Beth could see that the young man was anxious to talk to her about his unhappy state. She had planned to spend the rest of the afternoon working on her hair and makeup, but she owed Rick. He had been a good friend on the trail.

"Look, I have a few more items to pick up, but why don't you come over to my inn in a half hour or so, and we'll talk if you like."

Rick was grateful and said he would probably do just that, unless a job prospect interfered.

Beth was in her room unwrapping her purchases on the patchwork quilt of the elegant four-poster with its fishnet canopy when a rap sounded on her door. She went to answer it, fully expecting Rick. She was stunned when she opened the door to find Charles Hobart standing there in the passage, briefcase in hand.

Her first alarmed thought when she recovered from her surprise was that something had happened to Brian. "Did Brian send you?" she demanded hoarsely. "Is he all right?"

"My brother is perfectly well, Ms. Holland," he assured her quietly. "He's back in Georgia, but he'll join you this evening as planned. And, no, he didn't send me. In fact, he's not aware that I flew up here ahead of him and will be returning as soon as we've talked. May I come in?"

Beth hesitated and then moved aside in the doorway, inviting him to enter. Her mind was alive with questions as she closed the door after him. Why had he come? What did he want of her? Was this unannounced visit the explanation for Annie's last warning?

Charles was gazing at her, waiting for her to direct him to a chair. Beth remembered her manners with a hasty, "I think we can sit here." She indicated a pair of comfortable Windsor chairs facing each other across a low table in front of a homey Franklin fireplace.

Beth eyed him as they settled opposite each other, struck by the contrast between him and Brian. Now that she knew they were half brothers, it was surprising to realize how different they were. Charles, in his precise, gray business suit, was a colorless man with nothing of the warmth and easy humor that distinguished Brian.

Charles must have been using the same opportunity to observe her. The thin mouth smiled at her politely. "The trail life must agree with you, Ms. Holland. You're looking very fit. Or is there another reason for that glow you're wearing since I last saw you?"

What was he implying? She didn't trust him. "Why have you come to see me, Mr. Hobart?" She couldn't bring herself to call him Charles, maybe just because he was so pompously formal with her.

"To be honest with you," he answered her directly.

Beth was equally direct. "Haven't you been?"

"I wanted to be, right from the start. From the minute I realized the mistake I had made in accepting that challenge of yours, I wanted to be honest with you."

"Honest how?"

"I wanted to offer you a fair sum of money in exchange for dropping the hike."

Beth was appalled. "You meant to try to buy me off? And that's supposed to be honest?"

"It would have been straightforward, yes. But my brother insisted you weren't the type, that you would never go for it and that we had to use other tactics. I listened to him, but now I'm regretting it."

Beth felt herself going warm with indignation. "What are you suggesting? That Brian proposed some devious scheme to end my hike?"

Charles spread his hands in a gesture conveying inevitability. "Look at the facts, Ms. Holland. Could a co-owner of a company like Hobart easily afford to turn his back on his responsibilities to go off tramping in the wilderness for weeks, possibly months, on end? Why would he do that? Maybe because he has a certain, useful talent where women are concerned, and I think you've learned about that persuasive talent of his, Ms. Holland."

Beth shook her head angrily. "Save your breath, Mr. Hobart. I've already heard these arguments, and they don't impress me."

"Maybe because they weren't supported by any evidence. Until now," he added softly, reaching for the briefcase he had placed on the table between them.

Beth followed his hands unclasping the briefcase, a current of fear beginning to undercut her outrage.

Charles, holding the folder he had slid from the briefcase, gazed at her with a perceptive air. "Are you afraid to look at what I have here?"

Beth tried to maintain an impassive expression. "Of course not, but it isn't going to make any difference."

"We'll see." He opened the folder and laid a typescript in front of her on the table.

Beth glanced down at it. "What is that?"

"The engineer's report on the upcoming project in Maine. You can see here where Brian initialed it after scribbling a comment to the engineer. It indicates Brian was aware that the only viable spot for our development is between the two lakes. No other location will do."

Beth shook her head. "There are no surprises there."

"I realize that. I'm simply offering it as a concrete explanation for this." He held up a slip of paper. "And also this that follows it." He produced another typescript from the folder.

Beth held out her hand, but he withheld both documents. "Let me tell you what they are. The first one is a personal memo from Brian. It was written the day he first came to see you at your motel in Georgia. He gave it to one of the men on our downstate project who was heading back to Atlanta that morning. The memo was to be handed over to our staff at the home office."

Charles leaned forward and placed the slip of paper in her hand. Beth read it. The memo, unmistakably in Brian's hand, instructed certain Hobart employees to research Beth Holland, to learn all pertinent facts about her, including the personal ones.

Beth gave the directive back to Charles without a comment, but she was beginning to feel a little sick inside.

Charles went on. "This second typescript is the report that resulted from Brian's memo. It's not exactly an in-depth profile, considering the extremely limited time our people had, but it is adequate." He set the report in front of her. Beth, trembling a little, scarcely glanced at it. What it indicated was plain enough.

"There was a late-night emergency meeting at our Atlanta office the evening before you started on your hike," he said. "Brian came straight down from your motel to attend it. That was when he was given the report on you. The conference went on so long that it was necessary in the end to charter a helicopter to return him to the trail."

Brian had claimed he'd overslept at his hotel, Beth remembered, her hands trembling in her lap. Instead it appeared he had been down in Atlanta at a planning session regarding her.

Charles sat back in his chair, hands laced together. "Why do you suppose my brother needed to learn everything he could about you before he joined you on the hike?" he asked her calmly. "What was his motive, Ms. Holland?"

Beth glared at him, voice frosty. "I know what you're implying. That Brian was trying to discover my weak spots in order to... No, I'm not going to say it! It's despicable!"

He nodded. "I know, and I'm sorry. I can imagine what you're feeling. But the facts speak for themselves, don't they?"

Did they? This body of evidence that Charles had pressed on her was convincing, and she felt stricken by it, but she was not going to regard it as conclusive. She wasn't going to think the worst about Brian before he had the opportunity to explain himself. Anyway, she couldn't be in love with a man who would deliberately use her.

Then she remembered that there were other guys she'd fallen for. Ones who'd ended up either cheating or using her. But those were only infatuations, never the real thing like this. And no matter what people said, true love couldn't be that blind.

Beth faced Charles with a stubborn, "Just why have you come here, Mr. Hobart? You certainly didn't think I'd be so devastated by the contents of that briefcase that I'd be ready to terminate the hike here and now."

"I came," he said slowly, "because we've tried to handle this thing my brother's way, and it hasn't worked. Now I want to try it my way."

Beth laughed, an angry laugh. "The honest bribe, you mean?"

"It isn't a bribe," he insisted. He withdrew something else from his folder and held it out in front of her. "If you'll look at it, you'll see that this is a cashier's check. Not a sum to be paid to you but a direct donation to your Green

Guards, a contribution generous enough to enable the A.T. to build the causeway across that Maine swamp in a relocation of the trail. We could both win, Ms. Holland."

"You can call it what you like," she informed him coldly, "but I don't need it, and neither does the A.T. I'm winning that right-of-way with my hike, Mr. Ho—no, *Charles*—and I think that's exactly why you're here. You didn't expect I'd ever get this far, and now I'm more than halfway there, and you're so worried by it that you're desperate enough to try anything to defeat my hike."

"Yes," he agreed in a last bid to change her mind, "and your performance has been very impressive. But you have a long way to go yet, with all the worst New England hardships coming up. Wouldn't it be simpler to—"

"No!" Beth got decisively to her feet. "You came all this way for nothing, Charles! I'm going on, and if you're interested enough to be there, I'll see you in Maine!"

But her confidence deserted her the moment Charles reluctantly departed, and for the rest of the long afternoon, Beth alternated between hope and plain despondency. Not with regard to the hike itself. She still had the necessary courage and resolution to reach Maine, if only she could stop being in this turmoil about Brian.

She couldn't stop remembering how important the Maine project was to him and Hobart. Just how far would he go to save his development from any risk? To the extent of deliberately seducing her, getting her to actually fall in love with him, maybe even pretending to love her back if necessary? If she were to believe Annie and Charles, the challenge of Beth Holland wouldn't be difficult for him, not after his easy conquests of who knew how many other women before her. He *was* a practiced lover. All she had to do was recall that passionate night they had spent in the cabin to realize that.

But there was something else she remembered about that night: how deeply tender he had been. Could a man fake that sort of caring, *believably* fake it? And her knee... he had been so concerned about her knee, gently doctoring it. He hadn't needed to play it that way. For all he knew, the knee injury might have been serious enough to cancel her hike—a simple, convenient solution to Hobart's problem, providing he didn't help her to recover. Or had his treatment and worrying simply been part of the act?

Oh, Brian, I don't know what to believe until you're here with me! Hurry up and get here, please! I can't stand much more of this!

The mellow amber light of sundown was softly burnishing the creamy walls and polished oak floor of Beth's room when Brian finally arrived. She knew it was he at the door. No one else would rap with that cocky, insistent briskness. She went nervously to let him in, one half of her unable to contain her eagerness, the other half holding back, dreading the necessity of facing him with Charles's visit.

She caught her breath when she pulled the door back. She had forgotten how big he was. He filled the doorway with his powerful, rugged maleness. How she had missed him!

He stood, his long legs braced slightly apart, one hand holding a large carryall down at his side, the other hooked under the collar of a sport coat slung carelessly over one shoulder. A toothy grin slashed his bronze face above the familiar craggy jaw.

The blue-green eyes sparkled with his old wit. "Well, well, Yank, just look at you!"

"I've been shopping," she confessed, assuming he was referring to the new skirt and sweater.

His eyes widened with approval. "I can see, and it was damn smart shopping, too. Hey, do I get to come in, or do

I drag you out here and make a public spectacle of us in the hall?''

She moved aside, allowing him to stride impatiently into the room. She had scarcely shut the door after him and turned when, disposing of the carryall and coat on a chair, he was in front of her, reaching for her with a husky, hurried, ''How I missed you!''

His arms enfolded her in a tight embrace, his cheek caressing the side of her head. ''Your hair smells good,'' he murmured against her ear. ''Like the wildflowers out on the trail. I've been missing those, too.''

''I—it's grown out a lot. You'll have to cut it again.''

''Let me see.'' His strong hands reached up to frame her face. He gazed down intently for a long second, not at all interested in her hair. ''Yeah, we'll have to do something about it.''

He did. His mouth came down hungrily on hers. She was caught up in the flavor of him, the special taste and aroma that could only be Brian and no other. Their lips clung together with a long-denied ardor, but when he tried to deepen the kiss, he sensed, as he was always able to do, the faint restraint she was unable to help.

He held her away, puzzled. ''Whoa! What's this? It can't be my clothes. I was careful not to turn up in one of my wild outfits.''

Beth had noticed that right away—the crisp tan slacks above casual loafers, the maize-colored shirt open at the neck with sleeves turned back to expose a pair of sinewy, hair-darkened forearms. It was a potent combination, making his presence all the more irresistible, making it harder to say what had to be said.

''No,'' she admitted. ''It isn't the clothes.''

Arms dropping away from her, he frowned. ''You want to tell me what's up?''

Beth moved away from him, putting a safe distance between them. "Why don't we go down to the dining room? I'll tell you about it over dinner."

He followed her, stopping her at the door. "No, Beth, you tell me now. If there's a problem, I don't want our celebration dinner spoiled while we discuss it."

He was right. She turned around to face him, leaning back against the door, as though seeking support. "Charles was here," she informed him quietly. "He came this afternoon to show me what—what he had brought in his briefcase."

Brian listened without comment as she went on to describe the visit, but his expression turned grimmer by the moment. He heard her out, and then he cursed his brother savagely. "That damn fool! I'll break his neck for this!"

"Are you angry with Charles for flying up here without your knowledge?" she asked softly. "Or are you angry because I was told what I was never supposed to hear?"

He scowled at her, voice harsh. "My God, you believed him! You believed every word, didn't you?"

She shook her head. "I tried not to, Brian. But what am I supposed to think? I saw your directive and the report on me. They weren't invented by Charles, were they?"

"No, they weren't."

"And you were in Atlanta that night at a planning session with your staff after you left me at the motel?"

"I was."

"Well, then..."

He ran a hand distractedly through his tumbled brown hair. "Beth, don't you see that he took all that and twisted it around in order to convince you to accept his check?"

"But you did order an investigation on me, you did attend that meeting. Why?"

"I didn't know you at the time."

"And that's supposed to make it all right?"

"Yes. Look, Beth, it's not what you're thinking. There was nothing personal connected with it. Fact-finding is simply good business practice, and that's what I was doing."

"Arming yourself."

"*Preparing* myself. Damn it, there is a difference. And there was nothing dishonest about it. All I was doing was trying to learn just what Hobart was up against, something Charlie failed to do before he blundered into that wager with you."

"Learn what?"

"Things like exactly who you were, who your supporters were and how powerful they were, what prospects you had of actually completing the hike. There was never any scheme of using any of the information against you. Now, can you tell me that was so unfair, my simply wanting to know where Hobart stood in this thing, what our chances were?"

"Maybe not," she admitted. "But why didn't you tell me all this yourself? You could have told me that day we were sheltering from the rain in the cavern. You said then you were being open about everything, and you weren't."

"All right, it was wrong of me, but I wasn't sure yet about us. I'd already told you so much that day I was afraid to risk any more before I was positive just where we stood with each other. You were overwhelmed by what I did tell you, which was everything that mattered, so I figured the rest could wait because it didn't seem to matter."

"But I trusted you!" she cried.

"And I lied to you by omission. That's what you're saying, isn't it?"

"Yes."

"It's a two-way street, Beth."

"What does that mean?"

"Didn't you withhold from Charlie that day you walked into his office to propose your hike? He had no knowledge of the A.T., no idea that it was possible to walk from Georgia to Maine and that others had already done it."

"And I used his lack of knowledge to get him to agree to my hike, didn't I?" Beth sagged against the door in sudden self-reproach. "Oh, Brian, you're right! It *was* wrong of me, but he made me so mad with his arrogance, and I was desperate to preserve the right-of-way, and that's all I could see. But it doesn't make me any less guilty of taking advantage of him, does it?"

He lifted his hand, placing it comfortingly against the side of her cheek. "Yes, you were wrong, and I was wrong, but we weren't acting out of mean or selfish motives, Beth."

"But I went and blamed you when—"

"Shhh, no more self-recriminations. What's done is done. Let's start fresh from here."

"Yes," she agreed, nuzzling her cheek against the warmth and strength of his hand. "And no more surprises either, please. I can't take them. They hurt too much."

"No more surprises," he promised, trailing his fingers soothingly along the side of her jaw and across her parted lips.

Beth pressed her hand over his, capturing it against her mouth. Without conscious thought, she began to make love to his hand, gently nibbling his fingers one by one, stroking their slightly rough pads with the point of her tongue. Even here he tasted good. As she planted kisses against his palm, she heard him draw in his breath sharply in the first stages of arousal.

His hand left her mouth and slid to the back of her neck to draw her snug against him. She wilted against him readily, her mouth raised to his. Their kiss was a long, incendiary one of dueling tongues and small, eager whimpers.

Feeling all control slipping away from her, Beth drew her mouth from his. Her forehead dropped weakly against his breastbone where she could hear his heart thumping wildly. "Dinner," she reminded him in a dazed whisper.

"Later, sweetheart, later," he muttered urgently, and, bending, he scooped her up in his arms and carried her to the four-poster.

At the side of the bed, he lowered her to her feet long enough to free one hand to drag the quilt out of the way. Then, still supporting her around the waist, as though fearing he might lose her if he released her for even a second, he sank onto the bed, drawing her onto his lap where she could feel the hardness in his groin.

For a moment he simply held her, rocking her lovingly, and then he lowered his head, his mouth seeking her throat where he slowly lipped the tender skin, burying his nose in her fragrance, inhaling her.

His face when he lifted it was flushed, his eyes charged with desire. "Undress me," he commanded in a husky murmur. "I want to feel your hands on me. Everywhere."

"Yes," she complied without reservation, though she had never undressed a man before. Her trembling fingers fumbled with the buttons on his shirt. He was wearing nothing underneath, as if he had anticipated this moment. With the top buttons undone, she was able to slide her hands under his shirt, to freely explore the hot, hair-roughened flesh over slabs of hard muscle.

"Wait," he rasped.

She paused to allow him to shrug off the shirt and toss it aside. Then her hands renewed their travels, lingering over his flat nipples before passing down the V of curling hair to his waist. She felt his stomach muscles tense and tighten under her caressing fingertips before she encountered his belt and hesitated.

"Don't stop," he urged. "I want it all."

Sliding down his lap, she unhooked his belt, opened the snap on his trousers, lowered the zipper. Her hand squeezed inside his briefs where his tumescence sprang to life. She closed around him intimately, gripped, stroked.

Head back, Brian emitted deep, low grunts of pleasure. Then, struggling for control, he stiffened, uttering a ragged, "Easy, sweetheart, easy. Any more, and I won't be able to hold back. Here—" He guided her off his lap, giving himself the opportunity to kick off his shoes and to tug off his pants, briefs and socks. Then, magnificent in his nakedness, he reclaimed her, settling her again over his hard thighs.

He held her, kissed her, carefully building the forceful passion between them. Beth could not have said when her own garments were shed and she lay stretched back on the bed as Brian introduced a new dimension to their lovemaking.

He was suddenly everywhere at once, his inventive tongue possessing the taut peaks of her breasts, swirling over her sensitive navel, dipping lower, lower into the heart and fire of her womanhood until she was racked by wild shudders.

"Brian . . . Brian, *please*!"

She wasn't sure whether she was begging him to stop or to go on. He did heed her broken, moaned pleas but in a manner that was unexpected. Turning onto his back, his guiding hands conveyed a silent message, instructing her to position herself on top of him.

Beth amazed herself. Without hesitation or shyness, she lifted herself to her knees and straddled his hips. It felt natural. With this man, it felt right and natural.

"That's right, sweetheart," he husked. "Now help to guide me in."

Hand directing his hardness, she lowered herself on him slowly, filling herself with him until at last he was completely hers. A long, sighed, "Yes...oh, yes," expressed her pure satisfaction.

For a moment she was completely still with the wonder of it all. Then Brian stirred under her, squirming his impatience. "Don't stop now, sweetheart! Don't stop!"

Beth, adjusting herself with an enticing rotation of her hips that nearly sent him over the edge, began obediently to rock on him, building layer upon layer of rich, prolonged rhythms. Brian, straining upward, responded with deep, resonant groans, striving to match her quickening tempo.

The first shock waves struck her when, with a final burst of power, he thrust high, his body arching from the bed, a shout of triumph torn from him. Convulsions of pleasure were still sweeping through her as Beth collapsed against his sweat-dampened chest with an answering cry of radiant fulfillment.

They didn't see the dining room that night. Beth regretted neither the missed dinner nor the newly purchased outfit that never left the room. Their repeated lovemaking was all she wanted or needed.

Exhausted, she finally sank into a deep, blissful sleep. Brian did not sleep. Close beside her under the quilt, elevated with pillows under his shoulders, he looked down on her tenderly and with a growing sense of remorse. She didn't know how wholesomely beautiful and sexy she was. Her innate sense of modesty and her negative history with men permitted no vanity. She didn't know either just how deeply she affected him, how much he cared.

But he knew how she felt about him. Those warm brown eyes of hers were nearly always a giveaway, too honest not to betray to him her every thought and feeling. He was pretty sure she loved him, but he couldn't bring himself to tell her exactly what she meant to him. The was a reason—an internal struggle that had surfaced as his feelings for her had deepened.

He had promised her that there would be no more surprises, that he wouldn't hurt her again with any withheld secrets about himself. But you lied, you cowardly bastard. And so what if it isn't anything connected with the hike or the project in Maine, that it's entirely personal. It's still an omission, an important one. You'll lose her if you don't tell her.

But he just couldn't. No yet. He was too damned scared.

Eight

Beth was awakened several times in the night by Brian's restlessness. His turning and twisting made a disaster of the bed linens. She had to keep rescuing the quilt from the foot of the bed and once from the floor, drawing it back over their nude bodies, and then he would end up kicking it away again.

She hadn't known him to be an uneasy sleeper. Was he worried about something, having bad dreams? He did mumble something once, but he never woke up, and she didn't like to disturb him to ask.

The warm glow of morning was lighting the room when Beth, aware of her body's deep and utter contentment after last night's prolonged lovemaking, stretched languorously. She lifted herself on one elbow to check on the man responsible for her happiness. Brian was sleeping peacefully now.

She gazed down at him, a sweet, liquid sensation swelling inside her at the sight of him and at the memory of his tenderness the night before. A quality of boyish vulnerability in the way he was sleeping touched her. He was sprawled flat on his back. His bare feet stuck out below the bottom of the quilt, and his bare chest stuck out at the top. There was a stubble of beard on his strong chin, and he was snoring softly. This was the man she loved, and he was beautiful.

She was still admiring him when the phone rang on the bedside table. Brian didn't stir as she reached across him to answer it.

"Desk clerk, Ms. Holland. There's a Ms. James down here from the *Chronicle*. She says she has an appointment with you."

Oh, Lord, the reporter! She had forgotten all about that early-morning interview she had promised for the local paper at the A.T. Conference center yesterday.

"Tell her to have coffee on me in the dining room, breakfast if she likes, and I'll join her there in ten minutes."

Beth slid from the bed and headed for the bathroom where she had a lightning-quick shower and rushed into her clothes. When she was reasonably put together, she stopped beside the bed, wondering about leaving Brian.

She was leaning over him when he woke, smiled up at her sleepily and reached for her. "Morning, Yank," he croaked lazily.

"Morning yourself, Reb." She wanted nothing more than to submit to those outstretched arms and that splendid physique, but she was already late. "Sorry, but duty calls."

He seemed to realize then that she was up and dressed and about to depart. Scooting himself against the headboard, he scratched at his chest. "What's this?"

"In a weak moment yesterday I agreed to a newspaper interview this morning about the hike."

"This early?"

"Had to. Don't forget the trail is still waiting out there for us." He groaned. Beth laughed.

"Look," she suggested, "I'll just have a fast coffee with her. Why don't you order us a couple of breakfast trays up here, and we'll call it our celebration dinner?"

He grinned at her engagingly. "Yeah, we kind of missed that, didn't we?"

"I'm not complaining," she teased, "but I don't think you survived an empty stomach so well. You were flopping around all night. Was that hunger, or were you having nightmares?"

"Um—just restless, I guess," he answered vaguely. "Go before I change my mind and drag you back in here with me."

Considering the temptation and her own weakness where he was concerned, Beth fled from the room, leaving Brian reaching for the phone to order room service.

Beth didn't particularly care for Ms. James of the *Chronicle*. She was an attractive young woman with a striking mane of cinnamon-colored hair, but she had a catty way about her.

"You're getting a lot of attention out of this hike, aren't you?" she asked with arched eyebrows and a little smirk— as if she resented the publicity Beth was receiving, even though she was about to contribute to it herself.

"Yes," Beth admitted, "and I'm not comfortable with it, but since I hope it benefits the A.T., and maybe our environment in general, I don't object to it." She went on to credit Annie for her media campaign as she and Ms. James sat across from each other in a quiet corner of the inn's Victorian-style dining room.

Beth sipped her scalding coffee and tried to politely answer the reporter's questions. All the while she was eager to get back to Brian.

She was explaining some of the physical difficulties of the hike when Ms. James interrupted her impatiently, "That's all been well covered by now. What I'm looking for here is a fresh angle."

"Fresh how?"

The reporter leaned toward her eagerly. "Brian McArdle, one of the owners of Hobart Development, is hiking with you, isn't he?"

Beth wasn't sure she cared for the direction the session was taking, but she answered a truthful, "Yes."

"That's a rather unusual situation, isn't it?" the woman probed. "After all, you are on opposite sides in this battle."

Beth answered her carefully. "Mr. McArdle is monitoring the hike. He has that right."

"He doesn't trust you?"

"I didn't say that."

"You're a bit defensive about him, aren't you? Does that mean the speculations I hear are true and that the two of you did get romantically involved while you were out there on the trail together?"

The damn woman was looking for scandal, not facts! Beth restrained her displeasure, at least outwardly, and responded with a level, "I'm sorry, but that's strictly a personal matter and not for public consumption."

Ms. James, demonstrating that she meant to go far in her career, wasn't about to let the subject drop. "Is McArdle here with you at the inn?"

"Ms. James, I really don't see—"

"Or is the latest hot rumor correct, and he's gone back to Georgia?"

Now what was she insinuating? "What rumor?"

"That the two of you had a falling-out and have separated." She made it sound like a celebrity marriage on the rocks.

"We haven't had any 'falling-out,' as you put it. Why should we?"

There was the smirk again. "There might be a good reason for it if the story that recently appeared in a major Atlanta paper happened to come your way."

Beth, much against her will, was beginning to experience a distinctly uneasy feeling. "I don't know about any story," she said guardedly.

"I thought there was a chance you hadn't." The reporter opened her purse. "That's why I brought a copy with me. This came through our news service."

A photocopy of the dated Atlanta story was produced and handed to Beth. She read it with mounting dismay. The writer had apparently approached, and managed to briefly interview, both Brian and Charles as Brian was met by his brother at the airport the day he had flown back to Georgia. When asked to predict the outcome of Beth Holland's hike and the fate of the contested right-of-way, Brian was directly quoted with his claim that the conflict would soon be resolved to the satisfaction of both parties. How? He wasn't prepared at this time to say, but he was confident both Ms. Holland and the Green Guards would agree to a compromise that Hobart was soon to offer, thereby making any further pursuit of the hike unnecessary.

Beth felt sick. If the story was accurate, and she had no reason to suppose it wasn't, it indicated that Brian had not only been aware all along of his brother's errand here yesterday but had approved of it. Maybe he'd even authored it.

The compromise referred to was, of course, Charles's attempt to buy her off on behalf of Hobart. It had to be.

She tried to tell herself that she wasn't being fair, that she was jumping to conclusions.

But what else was she supposed to think? The evidence was so convincing.

It wasn't the hike that was in jeopardy this time, she realized. It was their relationship, and after last night . . . she couldn't stand it!

But she did stand it. She managed to return the photocopy of the story to Ms. James with a simple, "Thank you." No other reaction. Ms. James was clearly disappointed, both then and throughout the rest of the interview, which Beth somehow handled without betraying her anguish.

She knew, as she left the dining room and headed for her room, that it was probably a mistake facing Brian in her present state of turmoil. But she had no choice. He was waiting for her, and she had to see him. The whole conflict between them had to be settled, permanently settled this time, and without delay. She couldn't take any more of this emotionally exhausting, unending cycle of highs and lows.

She found Brian dressed and readying himself for the trail. He was crouched on the floor with his open carryall, loading his backpack with essentials and whistling softly. He looked up as Beth closed the door behind her. "You'll notice there are no breakfast trays," he reported cheerfully. "Seems the inn isn't into room service. We'll have to eat in the dining room, after all. So, how did the interview go?"

Beth didn't answer him. She remained where she was near the door, wondering how she was going to handle this. She felt all heavy inside.

Brian noticed her unhappy expression then. "Uh-oh, not so good, huh? What happened?"

She answered him indirectly with a flat statement. "Brian, I want to know why you were sleeping so restlessly last night."

He got slowly to his feet, the grin fading from his mouth. "What brought this on?"

"Was it—well, maybe because you were experiencing guilt over something just after we—after we made love?"

"Guilt over what?" he asked sharply. "What are you talking about?"

There was no other way to put it. "Because you lied to me. Because you promised there would be no more surprises when all along you were withholding another truth about yourself. Is that it?"

He tensed, and she could see the worry now in his expression. And the sudden wariness as well. It was true then! "Just what in hell did that reporter say to you?" he demanded grimly.

"She showed me a story that came through their news service. It appeared in one of the Atlanta papers." Beth went on to describe the contents of the report.

"And that's what you meant by my withholding something else from you?" She didn't notice the slow breath of relief he expelled nor the relaxing of his shoulders. She was too busy hurting. "You figured I lied to you yesterday and that I did know, after all, what Charlie was going to try to pull with that cashier's check."

"Well, isn't it true? Isn't that what I saw in your face just now?"

"What you saw in my face just now was—" No, he decided, this wasn't the time for a confession about some personal, internal struggle. Not with this other hanging over them.

"What, Brian?"

He crossed the room to where she was standing by the door, and he would have taken her hands, but she put them behind her back like a wounded child fearing the false persuasion of a treacherous adult. "No, Beth," he told her, trying to contain his rapidly building frustration, "the story is not true."

"But you were directly quoted."

"I can't help that. Look, there was a reporter there that morning at the airport. For all I know, Charlie arranged to have him there. I wouldn't put it past him. And I muttered some totally innocent, noncommittal comment about the hike, just to get the guy off my back. Then I went off to arrange a connecting flight for myself to the project downstate. Charlie waited for me, and that's when he must have fed the reporter all this junk about proposing a compromise. Probably, it was Charlie being important again and failing to use his head." Brian shrugged. "I suppose the reporter just assumed the stuff was coming from both of us. Why shouldn't he? I'm Hobart, too."

"But you were the one he quoted."

"Well, it was a mistake!" he snapped, his self-control fast sliding into a helpless anger. "Are you going to believe some damn news item rather than me?"

Beth gazed at him longingly, wanting and needing to believe him, but afraid to. She shook her head slowly. "I—I just don't know who or what to believe anymore, Brian. From the beginning, by your own admission, you misrepresented yourself, either withholding from me or omitting things. There's been all this—this game-playing, and now I just don't know what to trust."

She was expressing her desperate confusion to him, but in his own agitation of disappointment and exasperation he wasn't able to appreciate her position. "And that's what it all comes down to, doesn't it?'' he said rigidly. ''Trust. Because if we don't have that, Beth, we don't have anything.''

''That's not fair!'' she cried. ''I did trust you, and each time I did there was another bombshell dropped on me. I feel like my emotions have been on a wild seesaw ever since Georgia.''

He pinned his flinty gaze on her, he voice hard. ''Those bombshells wouldn't have counted, Beth, if you really cared about us and our relationship. You wouldn't keep on wondering if I'm capable of trickery and deceit. You'd have faith in the kind of man I keep trying to convince you I am. The kind of solid faith that's supposed to come out of what we shared last night.''

She stared at him, struggling for the absolute faith he demanded. But he wasn't telling her he loved her, he was offering no commitment at all, and without that . . .

Why go on pushing this? Brian wondered sourly, raking a hand wearily through his hair. She obviously didn't care for him with any of the same aching depth he cared about her. He had been wrong last night in thinking that she did. Otherwise, she would have indicated it by now.

Beth stood there, meeting his angry gaze and remembering that time in the cavern when they had sheltered from the rain. She had wanted Brian to go back to his work in Georgia, fearing more blows if he went on with her. It was a mistake, my listening to him, she thought bitterly. I should have gone on alone. At least that way I could have preserved my precious illusions.

''That's right, Beth,'' Brian said. ''Why go on punishing ourselves? Maybe it is better to leave it here.''

His words startled her. Had she just spoken her careless thoughts aloud without realizing it, or was he really able to read her that deeply? *You're frightening me, Brian! I didn't mean it! I don't want us to separate, not now or ever!*

"What are you saying?" she asked, her voice so cold with fear it was unable to express her actual emotions.

That cold voice told him everything. Yes, he thought, all considered, it's for the best. He had these tormenting feelings that he had to work on before he could ever risk committing to another woman. Until he overcame those old fears, it wouldn't be fair asking her to stay with him. Not now, anyway, with the way she was feeling about him. Maybe never. But how was he going to stand not having her beside him?

"Brian?"

He didn't want her to see how heartsick he was, how he was being pulled apart inside. "What I'm saying," he told her harshly, biting the words in an effort not to betray himself, "is that I'm just as tired as you are of this emotional seesaw."

So he was deserting her! She was devastated over his intention. "Fine!" she shouted hatefully. "Just fine! I'll go on with the hike alone! I can make it on my own, you know!"

She was flinging the words at him like a challenge. The little scar over his left eyebrow turned a livid white against his flushed skin. "That's right, Beth," he said softly. "You've proved you don't need anyone out there on the trail. That's the way you've always wanted it anyway, isn't it? On your own. Well, you've got it!"

He swung away from her, collected his carryall and backpack from the floor and strode past her out the door. He left without another word, without any indication that he would see her after Maine. He was gone, and Beth was alone in the sudden, awful silence of the room.

* * *

She found herself sinking into one of the Windsor chairs, her legs unable to support her. Her mind was numb with shock and a profound despair.

How did it happen? It was all so fast. One minute she and Brian were standing here talking to each other, and the next minute he was out of her life. How could it end like that?

But what did she expect after the destructive things she'd said to him? She'd actually yelled at him. Why wouldn't he want to get away after that?

But it was all so abrupt, and nothing was settled.

It was settled all right. She'd settled it by sending him away, and she was going to have to live with that for a long time to come.

But not like this. Not sitting here wallowing in grief. Get up and get on with it, she told herself.

It was a sound piece of advice, and she obeyed it, struggling to her feet. The realization that she must move on without Brian chilled her. She couldn't imagine his no longer being there beside her as he had been from the start. She would be lost without him. But there was no question of her not continuing the hike. It had to be done, not just for the benefit of the Appalachian Trail but for herself as well. They said that walking the trail could heal all manners of distress, all the negatives of the human condition. Well, now she would see for herself.

Collecting her gear, she left the room, checked out at the desk and stopped at the dining room. She was all hollow inside, and though food couldn't fill the emptiness, she had to eat something after missing dinner last night. The practical couldn't be ignored. She needed to maintain her energy for the waiting trail.

Beth was choking down a breakfast of cold cereal and toast when Rick Hansen found her with a breathless, "They said at the desk that Mr. McArdle left for the airport. Does that mean he won't be going on with you, after all?''

She made herself answer the young man in a steady voice. "That's right, Rick. There's been a change in plans."

"With me, too." He turned a chair around and straddled it, leaning toward her eagerly. "That's what I stopped by to tell you. I'm going to be able to go on with the hike."

Beth was surprised. "I thought you had to stop over here and find work."

"No, it's all okay now. I called my folks. We had a real good talk, and this time they listened. We made a deal. They wired me enough money to finish the hike, and I promised that I'd go back to Ohio afterward and start college in the fall."

"That's great, Rick."

"Yeah, it is. Look, since you're going on without Mr. McArdle, would you mind if I tagged along again? Be safer that way."

Beth looked at his thin, earnest face with the sense of boyish adventure in his blue eyes and thought, why not? Rick's good company, and maybe he'll help me not to miss Brian so much.

But it didn't work out that way. As they headed north through a corner of Maryland and on into Pennsylvania, Beth felt as lonely as though she were completely on her own. She didn't just miss Brian. That would have been easy. But she'd been left with this withering, worthless sensation inside, as though she were lacking half of something meant to be whole. She had lost more than just a lover. She had lost her best friend, the compatible someone who knew her more intimately than she knew herself, who understood and shared her innermost feelings.

Oh, but what was the use of regrets? She had only herself to blame. She had driven him off with her constant mistrust. He had had enough, and he had walked out. Simple as that.

But if he hadn't been using her for the sake of Hobart Development Company, then wouldn't he have stayed and tried to work it out if he loved her? She realized all over again, only with greater clarity this time, he'd never indicated that he *did* love her. Yes, he had cared but seemingly never in the way she did. All along she must have been building their special togetherness into something that was totally one-sided, a miracle he didn't share.

The likelihood of this haunted her in the long weeks that followed, but it didn't prevent her from punishing herself with a series of poignant memories.

Traveling through the peaceful Amish farmlands, she recalled Brian's appreciation of a simple country life-style and imagined how much he would have enjoyed this region. She could even hear the observations he would have made in his lazy drawl about the Amish buggies and the Dutch barns.

When they crossed the state line into New Jersey and the trail passed along a field where a local fair was in progress, Beth and Rick paused to listen to an old man playing country music on a saw. Brian's brand of music. The saw would have evoked his deep, rich laughter. He would have lingered to talk to its player. She missed his ease with strangers and his playful humor the most. The longing was a bittersweet one, cutting painfully into her resolve to put him out of her mind. But how was she to achieve that when she kept stumbling over his grinning ghost?

Her senses went on a real rampage when, in a shelter somewhere in New York state, while searching for her sewing kit in the depths of her backpack, she found wadded up at the bottom of a compartment one of Brian's tank tops. How it had ever wandered into *her* pack she had no idea, but she was shaken by the discovery. She sat there with the garment in her lap, fingering the dark blue cotton, conjuring up an image of the hard, sexy body that had worn it. The tank top, when she held it to her face, still bore the faint, distinctive aroma of the man she loved.

For a long moment she savored his male scent, and then she carefully returned the top to her pack. She ignored the wisdom of either throwing it away or laundering it. She couldn't. In the physical sense, it was all she had left of Brian, and she needed to keep it close to her.

But why did she go on tormenting herself with these excessive cravings, inflicting anguish on herself with every turn in the trail, when there was this hopeless divide between them and no sign of a bridge that could cross it?

Harpers Ferry was an eternity ago. Since leaving it, Brian had made no effort whatever to communicate with Beth. He could have, if he had cared to, because she regularly passed along her progress and whereabouts to Hobart through Annie.

It was Annie, in one of their phone calls, who bluntly told her, "You sound like hell."

"I'm fine," Beth insisted.

"Hah! You're in love with him, and it's killing you. Look, maybe I was wrong about him, Beth. Maybe he's an okay guy, after all. Why don't you call him? I bet he'd fly up if you asked. You could settle this whole thing."

"There's nothing to settle, Annie."

No, she couldn't call him. She couldn't face another rejection. Maybe after the hike. Maybe then. But right now she needed all her strength and courage for the difficult trail, though everyone seemed to be accusing her of losing it.

Even her mother expressed her concern. "You don't sound well, Beth. Are you sure you're all right?"

"I'm all right, Mom."

"I don't think you should be out there anymore. It's too strenuous, all these weeks and weeks of tramping up and down the country."

It drove Beth wild having these well-meaning people on her back, having to calmly and repeatedly assure them of her fitness when, emotionally anyway, she felt anything but fit.

Thank God for Rick. He was an undemanding companion, never questioning her moods, and he saved her from complete forlornness. When he was there, that is. During the dull, easy sections of the trail, he would disappear for several days at a time, chasing off like a happy puppy to investigate the towns and side trails that Beth had no time for since she had to faithfully cover every mile of the main trail. Hitching rides, the young man always managed to catch up with her again, seemingly appearing out of nowhere with his inevitable, amiable, "How's it going?" He would tell her then what he had seen on his side trips or talk about his girl back in Ohio, and later he would vanish again on another carefree exploration.

But Rick always managed to be with her during the worst ordeals of the trek, and in New England these were absolutely brutal. In Connecticut her hiking shoes fell apart, just as Brian had predicted they would long ago in the South. A new pair she purchased threatened to raise blisters that might defeat her hike when nothing else could. Rick somehow secured her a sound but comfortable used pair of shoes in her exact size.

In Massachusetts, they suffered an infestation of black flies so vicious that they had to muffle their heads with sweaters. In the Green Mountains of Vermont they fought through a violent thunderstorm and sweltering summer heat. In New Hampshire, they survived the blasting, icy winds of Mount Washington. But nothing was so cruel as Maine's notorious Mahoosuc Notch, where the trail wound through a steep-walled channel so narrow and harsh that in places the only way she and Rick could squeeze through the overhanging boulders was on hands and knees, dragging their packs behind them.

Through it all, through every drastic hardship and angry obstacle, Beth managed to preserve her determination and endurance, urging herself toward the trail's end in northern Maine.

Summer was on the wane, the Queen Anne's lace thick in the meadows. Rick was off on another side jaunt when Beth, all alone on the trail, arrived at the land between the two lakes. So here it was, the beautifully forested acreage where Hobart was to locate its luxury resort and what the contest of wills between Brian and her was all about.

Oh, Brian, Brian, why did it have to be this place that brought us together and then pulled us apart? Because what started over this land is ending over this land, and I don't know how I'm going to live with that. Or without you.

Inhaling deeply, as though the sharp, pine-scented air might bring her some measure of fortitude, Beth made herself stroll around the clearing where her Uncle Ray's summer camp had once stood. But the buildings had all been razed long ago, and nothing seemed familiar anymore. The gleaming, pure waters of Lake Sweetwater were as inviting as she remembered, though, and she went down to the shore and sat on a sagging old pier where she heard the loons and watched a moose come to drink. Would the loons and the moose still come here after Hobart built its project? She hoped so.

There was no sign as yet of the development to come, no sounds or stir of humanity. She had the place to herself. But she didn't linger there for very long. There was something sad and lonely about it. Beth moved on.

On the second day after leaving the land between the two lakes, topping a rise, she had her first view of Mount Katahdin looming in the distance. There, atop that massive shoulder of granite, the Appalachian Trail ended. This was it then, what she had struggled through two long seasons and two thousand miles to reach. She would make it now, but then she had never doubted from the start that she would.

With her goal at last in sight, she should have been brimming with exhilaration, but she couldn't seem to summon the excitement the occasion demanded. Well, it had been a long and arduous two thousand miles, and she was tired. Still, if Brian had been beside her now, sharing the moment...

He isn't, so forget it. Come on, you're almost there.

Well, not quite. She knew from her maps and guide that the base of Mount Katahdin was almost two days ahead.

Rick had not reappeared by midmorning of the second day, when she reached Baxter State Park, the gateway to Katahdin. But she didn't worry about him. He could take care of himself, and he would probably turn up for the final climb to the summit.

She was several miles short of Pitman Campgrounds, where she would rest before making the ascent, when a helicopter swooped down over the forest and seemed to follow her along the trail.

Beth didn't appreciate this noisy escort, but she forgot all about the chopper as she came through the trees and discovered the bewildering reception waiting for her in the campground clearing.

Nine

They had gathered at the point where the trail emerged from the forest. When Beth appeared they surged toward her in a clamorous mass, surrounding her, calling out congratulations, applauding what they already regarded as her triumph. Cameras were pointed at her, among them a TV camera and a mike was thrust into her face.

"Connie Devlin, Channel 6 News!" someone at her shoulder introduced herself above the uproar. "Can you tell us what you're feeling at the very special moment, Ms. Holland?"

What she was feeling? All she was feeling was shock! After her long solitude on the trail, this rush of blurred humanity was like a terrifying ambush. Beth couldn't answer the reporter. She could only stand there and gape.

To her immense relief, a lanky, very bald man squeezed his way through the crowd and came to her rescue, dispatching the mike and camera tactfully but firmly. "I'm sure Ms. Holland will be happy to answer all questions when she meets with the media in the picnic shelter, but right now she must be overwhelmed." He turned to Beth with a genial handshake, introducing himself. "I'm Frank Rosinski, Ms. Holland, local rep for the Green Guards. Welcome to Baxter State Park. Sorry about all the fuss, but we're very proud of you, and of course the Green Guards are as pleased as punch."

Beth managed to find her voice, muttering a dazed, "Who are all these people? Where did they come from?"

"Campers mostly. The word spread fast that you were about to arrive, and they collected to cheer you on in."

"But it's premature," Beth objected. "I still have five more miles to go to the top of Katahdin where the trail officially ends."

"Oh, that's just a formality, and you couldn't expect them to climb up there with you to celebrate."

"Yes . . . well, I'm flattered, but—"

"Don't say it." He held up one hand, grinning. "You're not just another two-thousand-miler, Ms. Holland. In this particular instance, your conquering of the trail is a kind of victory for all of us."

"And the newspeople—"

"Yes, they've descended on us, too. But that was arranged for in advance. I believe you called Atlanta at your last stopover to report you were almost here."

Annie! What had her friend gone and done to her now?

But as Frank Rosinski revealed with his next words, it wasn't Annie who had assembled the media this time. "He flew up from Atlanta to be here on the spot. He's waiting for you over in the picnic shelter where they're all set up."

Beth felt suddenly light-headed with anticipation. "Who?" she asked him eagerly.

"Why, the fellow from Hobart."

"Then the helicopter brought him?" Hope soared as she remembered how another helicopter had once delivered Brian to her side on the trail.

"No, he didn't come in on that. That's a cable-news chopper. They went up to scout out your exact where-abouts, and that's how the word was radioed back that you were on your way in. Actually, I believe that Mr. Hobart arrived from the airport early this morning in a rented RV."

"Mr. Hobart?" she asked weakly.

"Right, Charles Hobart himself. I know. We were sur-prised, too. You okay, Ms. Holland?"

"I—yes, I'm fine." Beth struggled to hide her massive disappointment.

"You're tired," the Green Guards representative said kindly. "And that's understandable. It's been a long haul, and then we go and throw all this at you. Come on up to the picnic shelter. You can rest there before you face that last climb."

The well-wishers parted at Frank's urging, allowing them access to the footpath that ascended to the shelter. Beth, still in a state of confusion, was led away from the commotion. Charles here! What was it all about? And Brian...where was Brian? Probably still back in Georgia. Why should he be here? But then why should Charles, either?

They came in sight of the open-sided shelter, and Beth saw that she was to trade one tumult for another. The place was packed with newspeople waiting to interview her. Charles slipped from the group and came forward to meet her.

More surprises then. This was a Charles Hobart she had never seen. He was smiling, actually looking gleeful, and he greeted her with an effusive warmth. "I know I'm not the first to offer my congratulations, but I hope I'm among the happiest to see you here at last safe and sound."

This didn't make sense. Charles Hobart pleased to see that she had conquered the trail? What was going on here?

"I'll turn you over to Mr. Hobart now," Frank said, "but I'll be standing by if you need me."

Beth thanked him and then turned to Charles. "Could you please explain—"

"Take off that backpack, why don't you? You'll feel better without it. You must be ready to drop."

"No, I—"

But he was already helping her to remove the backpack, fussing around her happily. "I'll carry it for you. Come on into the shelter. They're waiting to ask you a few questions. I hope you won't mind. You can sit, and there are refreshments."

"Refreshments!"

"Why, yes. A table with catered hors d'oeuvres and champagne to toast your victory."

This was crazy. She felt like Alice in Wonderland. A very baffled Alice in Wonderland. "Charles, I want to know what this is all about. Why are you here like this when—"

"Later, later. Let's not keep the press waiting any longer. They're getting anxious."

Against her will, she was led to a bench at one end of the shelter, and for the next twenty minutes she faced a barrage of cameras and questions. Charles was in his element with the media, circulating among them with a liveliness that in no way resembled the stuffy manner Beth remembered. What on earth had happened to bring about this change? Why was she no longer the enemy but suddenly the much favored ally?

Finally, unable to endure her perplexed state any longer, or another question from the news force, Beth called a halt to the interview and sought out Charles at the refreshment table. "Now, if you don't mind," she demanded, "I would like some answers. Actually, quite a few answers."

Charles, for the first time, looked a trifle awkward, glancing around at the newspeople. Frank Rosinski, who was still with them as promised, understood and stepped forward. "I have an office at my disposal in the park headquarters just over here. You're welcome to use it if you'd like a bit of privacy."

Charles said he would appreciate that, and the Green Guards rep led them along to the nearby office where he left them alone together, closing the door. Beth, thankful for the quiet retreat, leaned against the corner of the scarred desk and faced Charles, waiting for his explanation.

Clearing his throat rather noisily, he offered an apology. "First of all, I hope you'll forgive me, Beth, for any—uh—well, past differences we might have had. They weren't intended personally, you understand."

"I understand." Did she? No, of course not. "But your flying up here like this, and all that out there—" She waved her hand in the direction of the picnic shelter. "Why?"

"Well, of course, we wanted to be on hand for the completion of your hike, both of us, but—"

"We?"

"Why, yes, Brian is with me. He's waiting down in the RV for all this stir over your arrival to clear off. He doesn't like to involve himself with the public side of the business if he can help it, but I think you know that. Your young friend Rick Hansen was with him when I left him."

"Rick is here, too?" This was growing more complicated by the moment.

"That's right. He came in about an hour ahead of you. Hitched a ride here, I believe."

But Beth wasn't listening to that part. All she really cared about was that Brian had come, after all, and was close by.

Her heart lifted and then dropped with Charles's next words.

"As I say, we wanted to be here for your arrival, but we're also here to work. Now that this controversial hike has ended and everything is satisfactorily settled, we'll be meeting with the engineers at the Sweetwater site in order to get this project underway. That's why we've rented the motor home. It's to be our headquarters for a couple of weeks down there."

So Brian had come only for that, not her. He was here to work on the project. Had she mattered at all, he would have been on hand with the others to welcome her. A dull misery settled over Beth.

"You might want to join us at the site," Charles was saying, too enthusiastic to notice her despondency. "We'll have to determine just how and where the A.T. will come through the project, and with your experience . . . well, your advice would be appreciated."

Whatever you're feeling, Beth, the hike and the purpose behind it still matter. You can lick your wounds later, but right now . . .

Calling on her reserve of determination, she cut Charles short. "Just a minute. Are you telling me that the right-of-way is to be preserved in its present location, that it's no longer a subject of dispute, even though I have yet to complete the hike?"

"Exactly."

"And you're actually pleased to donate that right-of-way. That's been obvious since the picnic shelter. Why?"

Charles, for the first time, looked slightly embarrassed. "It seems that Hobart's careful research has missed the mark with this development. Our survey indicated that a resort of this nature demanded privacy on every level, but all the recent publicity over your hike has produced a reverse reaction. Regarding the trail itself, that is. Instead of objecting to the A.T. on their doorstep, our prospective, health-conscious buyers seem to consider it a distinct advantage. We've already had a load of interested inquiries, even two offers to purchase.''

Now it all made sense! No wonder there was this complete change in Charles's attitude. It also explained why he had gathered the newspeople. More free publicity for the project.

"So, you see,'' he went on, "we both end up benefiting from your hike.''

"But the hike isn't finished yet,'' she pointed out.

"Oh, that isn't necessary now. They tell me it's a rather grueling climb up there, and you ought to save yourself from it. Besides, it'd be a bit anticlimactic at this point, I think.''

The office door had opened quietly while they were talking, and neither of them had noticed. Not until Brian spoke were they aware of his arrival.

"What were you telling her just now, Charles?''

Beth's gaze flashed to the doorway at the familiar sound of that deep, mellow voice. Heart in her throat, she stared at him longingly, struck by the difference in him. He was still the solid, rugged male who could affect her senses almost violently by his mere appearance, but this wasn't the Brian she remembered.

At first, she thought it was because he was wearing a dark blue, three-piece business suit. His shock of thick hair was, for the first time since she had known him, trimmed back close to his temples, its waywardness actually tamed. He was impressively handsome like this, except it somehow didn't suit him. But, no, she decided, it wasn't the clothes or the haircut that made him unfamiliar. It was his attitude as he stood there in the doorway.

The Brian McArdle that Beth had known out on the trail had been fun-loving, entirely open in his nature, and even that last time when they had parted at the inn in Harpers Ferry, when he had been so angry with her, he had still been the man she loved and wanted. But this Brian was someone else. He stood there, tall and military-erect, and his whole manner, his cool expression, his even voice, spoke of a complete detachment. He frightened her, this remote stranger. Frightened her deeply.

"Oh, Brian," Charles said cheerfully, unaware of her sudden wilting at the desk. "You're finally here. I was wondering when you would tear yourself away from poring over those specs to join us."

"What were you telling her?" Brian persisted.

"Just that it isn't necessary for her to cover those last demanding five miles to the top of Katahdin. Help me to persuade her, Brian, that the trail ends here for her."

Beth waited for him to turn his head and look at her, willing him to direct his attention her way. If she could look straight into his eyes, perhaps she would know what he was feeling in this moment, whether there was any warmth at all in those blue-green depths, pure ice, or—possibly nothing. But his gaze remained fixed on Charles.

"Why?" he demanded in a level voice. "Isn't she in condition to make the last leg of the hike?"

"Of course I am," Beth insisted, hoarse voice betraying her hurt and anger that he should be asking this of Charles and not directly of her.

"That's not the point," Charles argued. "She doesn't have to climb up there, so why should she? It's all been settled now."

Brian was briefly silent, and then he said with perfect ease and firm decisiveness, "I'm afraid I disagree with you, Charlie. As far as I'm concerned, the agreement between

Hobart Development and Beth Holland is still in effect. If this wager is to be satisfied, she goes to the end of the trail. Every step of the way. And I intend going with her myself to see that she does just that. I think I have that right."

Beth was stricken by his demand. He didn't trust her! He was not only insisting that she go to the absolute end, he meant to personally accompany her to see that she did honor the agreement. Why did he hate her so much?

Charles, flustered, was prepared to object, but they were interrupted at this point by one of the park rangers. He had been at the counter in the outer office, and now he poked his head around the door that Brian had left open behind him. "Sorry, but did I hear you folks just now planning to climb Katahdin?"

"That's right," Brian answered.

The young ranger shook his head. "Afraid not. In case you've been too busy to look outside and notice, a fog has closed in. The mountain is all in clouds, like it is half the time. That's a tough climb. You can't try it until this stuff clears. Wouldn't be safe."

Brian nodded. "I see. In that case, we wait." He looked at Beth then for the first time, but to her mortification, the glance that flicked over her seemed to be one of utter disinterest. "In the meantime," he informed her flatly, "I'm heading back to the RV to change my clothes. You'll find me there working when you're ready."

If there was any meaning in the brief, last look he directed her way, she failed to comprehend it because his expression as he turned and left the office was still an unemotional one, as though he no longer cared about her either way. His abrupt departure sent a chill through Beth's heart. She realized now that he didn't hate her, but she would have preferred his hate to this devastating indifference.

There was silence then in the office. Charles, sensing at last that all wasn't quite as perfect as he wanted it to be, murmured uncertainly, "I—suppose I'd better get back to the shelter and try to keep the newspeople happy. I think some of them were planning to hang around in case you did decide to go the last distance, and they could cover that aspect of it. I wonder how long fogs last around here?" Beth had no answer for him. He moved restlessly toward the door. "Are you coming with me?"

She shook her head. "No, I'll wait here." She was in no mood to deal again with reporters.

He nodded and left her. When he was safely gone, Beth followed him outside. She didn't want to stay in the office either. She was better off out in the open where she could breathe.

She stood on the flagged walk and surveyed the landscape—what little she could see of it. The fog had moved in off the mountains with a surprising swiftness, shrouding the trees, veiling the nearby lawns and flower beds. Somewhere in its grayness a mourning dove called softly, and she thought how its depressing sound matched her spirit of the moment.

Then there was another call, a human one. "Beth?"

She turned her head. A few paces along the path, ghost-like in the fog with his blondness, Rick sat on a bench. She moved to join him.

"I was waiting for you to come out," the thin young man said, tugging at his curly beard. "I wanted to say goodbye."

Beth sat beside him on the bench. It was slightly damp from the fog, but she ignored that. Her mind was on Rick's last words. "Goodbye? You're leaving?"

He nodded. "Yeah, there's a camping party packing up and heading out in a little bit. They promised to give me a ride to the bus station in town."

Beth was astonished. "But aren't you going to wait to climb Katahdin? It's just a few more miles to the end of the trail, and when you've come all this distance . . ."

He shook his head. "No, I don't need to prove anything like that to myself. That isn't why I walked the trail, just so I could get to some official end like you have to. I decided I've hiked long enough. Anyway, I miss my folks." He grinned at her sheepishly. "Well, maybe I miss my girl more."

She nodded understandingly.

"Besides," he added, "it's not like you need me out there anymore."

"Need you?"

"Well, sure. Brian told me he's going to the top with you, so you'll have him."

"Oh, yes."

Rick paused, this time pulling nervously at his denim jacket. "Look, Beth, there is another reason I wanted to see you before I left. I've been feeling a little guilty, and I kind of wanted to apologize about that."

"Guilty? Why?"

"Well, you know. For lying to you about the reason I was with you on the trail."

Beth stared at him. "No," she said slowly, "I don't know."

Rick lowered his blue gaze in sudden embarrassment. "Brian was with you in the office just now, so I assumed he told you all about it. He said he was going to tell you at the end. I guess maybe I spoke out of turn then. I'd better shut up about it."

"No, Rick," she insisted, "I want to know what this is about."

"But, look, if I—"

"Please."

He looked indecisive for a moment, then nodded. "Okay, I guess you're entitled. Remember back in Harpers Ferry when I told you at the inn that my folks wired me money so that I could continue the hike?"

"Yes."

"Well, that wasn't the truth. The truth is, Brian looked me up that morning on his way to the airport and offered to finance the rest of my hike if I would stick with you on the trail."

Beth was incredulous. "He *paid* you to accompany me?"

"Yeah, so I would be there with you over the tougher sections, just in case you got into trouble. For the easier stuff, we decided I could take off for some side exploring. I guess he thought you might get suspicious if I was so obviously there with you every step of the way, even though I was with you all the time on the haul before Harpers Ferry."

"Wait a minute. Are you saying he also recruited you that first time down at Rita's farm?"

"Well, yeah. Otherwise, I really couldn't have afforded to go on with the hike."

No wonder Rick's animosity toward Brian had overnight turned into an eager friendliness! "But why? Why wasn't I told about this—this little conspiracy?"

Rick shrugged. "Brian said you might not accept me if you knew he'd arranged to have someone there for you, especially someone he was hiring to play, well, kind of a bodyguard. But maybe he also didn't want anyone to know he was paying somebody for what amounted to helping out the other side."

Beth's head was spinning with this newest mystery. If Brian had arranged for Rick to look out for her all these weeks, to help her toward a goal that actually went against Hobart's interests at the time, then why was he insisting now that she complete the hike when it was no longer necessary to prove anything?

Rick was watching her anxiously. "You're not mad at me, are you, Beth? I mean, I didn't do it for any profit. The money was only to keep me going. That's all I wanted, and Brian agreed to that. Well, bus fare home, too. But I did want to walk with you because I believed in what you were doing, and that was the important part of it, I promise."

"No," she said quietly, "I'm not angry, Rick." She got decisively to her feet. She needed answers suddenly. A lot of answers. And she wasn't going to get them from Rick. There was only one man who could supply her with the explanations her heart and mind burned to know. "Rick, where do I find this RV that Brian is holed up in?"

"Along the path there. It's not far. They got it parked in a grove down there. It's so big you can't miss it, even in this fog." He stood beside her. "I guess this is so-long then, huh?"

"Yes." She hesitated and then reached out to hug him briefly. "Thanks, Rick, for being there for me. You might not realize it, but you helped with your company a lot more than you ever helped with any bodyguarding. You let me hear from you. I want to know how everything turns out when you get back to Ohio."

He smiled at her with his engaging shyness. "I think

maybe all right. See, I've decided when I go back to school that I'll study ecology. Hey, you've been an inspiration!''

They hugged again, and then Beth, no longer able to wait, hurriedly left the bench. Not daring to hope, but hoping just the same, she began to walk eagerly, fearfully down the long hill in the direction of the RV.

Ten

Spreading maple trees, already wearing the first tints of autumn, sheltered the long, sleek motor home. There was no one around. The grove, wrapped in fog, was a quiet island as Beth approached the RV, the constriction in her throat evidence of her turbulent emotions.

She found the vehicle's main door left slightly ajar, like an invitation. Was it an invitation? She lifted her hand, hesitated, then rapped resolutely on the cold metal.

"Come on in, Beth."

His confident, immediate answer from somewhere beyond the door surprised her. How did he know it was her? He hadn't been looking through a window. Swinging the door wide, she climbed into the RV. She noticed with a glance that the interior was impressive, fitted with every modern convenience.

Brian was seated in the compact dinette off the entry. The specifications for the development were spread out on the table in front of him, but a notepad at his elbow covered with a jumble of doodles indicated that he hadn't been concentrating very successfully on his work.

He came slowly to his feet with her entrance, and she breathed a little easier when she saw that he had exchanged the intimidating business suit for his familiar jeans and a crewneck sweater that emphasized the breadth of his shoulders.

"How could you be so sure it was me out there?" she asked him, wishing she sounded as casual as he now looked, though his gaze meeting hers directly for the first time was not casual. There was something strained in his eyes.

Brian frowned over her words. "I've been waiting for you. Wasn't it agreed that you would join me down here?"

"Yes, when the fog had cleared and I was ready to begin the climb, but you must have noticed that there isn't a sign yet of the fog lifting."

"But that isn't what I meant in the office when I—" He stopped and shook his head.

"What?" she questioned him sharply. "What did you mean?"

"Just that I thought you understood," he muttered. Which, obviously, she doesn't, he realized, shoulders slumping in disappointment. Damn her, why does she have to sound so self-controlled about it all when I'm being ripped apart inside over this thing? And look at her! Weeks and weeks of roughing it out in the wilderness, brown as a nut, her hair in that awful braid again, her clothes a mess, and she sails in here still managing to look like a pint-size sex goddess. Tough and fragile all at the same time, and, God, I want her, and if she doesn't want me— How am I going to make her listen? What am I going to say to make her understand just how it has to be with us?

"No, Brian," she told him with a careful levelness in her voice, "I don't understand at all."

"It's just that we couldn't talk up in that office. There was no privacy there with all those people standing around. I thought I was letting you know that we could talk down here without being disturbed."

"Brian, it sounded more like a dismissal than an invitation."

"I'm sorry if that's how it came out. The thing is, this is—difficult for me." He reached around her to draw the door shut. "Look, there are sodas and food in the refrigerator. Can I get you anything?"

She shook her head. "I don't want anything."

"Well, sit down, anyway."

There were sofas facing each other across the narrowness of the camper. Beth settled in one, and Brian perched opposite her. The space was tight between them, and their knees almost touched as he hunched toward her. She wasn't sure this was wise. They were closed in here together now, and she was much too aware of his potent nearness, and what if—oh, damn, the tightness was still there in her throat, but this had to be dealt with. No more delays.

She lifted her gaze to meet his, and she was astonished. He suddenly looked awkward and unsure of himself, not the Brian of less than an hour ago nor even the Brian she had known out on the trail, though there was a familiar grimness around his mouth. What had he meant by those words "difficult for me"? They sounded so ominous, like a man ready to permanently end a relationship.

"I guess we do have to talk," she agreed hoarsely. "There are things I need to know."

"Yes?" he encouraged tensely.

She didn't intend to rush her words, but she found herself doing exactly that. "I left Rick just a minute ago. He told me what you went and did. That you hired him to stick with me on the trail. That I wasn't to know anything about it."

"And you're angry. You don't think I had any business seeing to it that you were protected out there."

"Maybe I have a right to be. Maybe I'm outraged because there was this male conspiracy to make sure that the helpless little woman was looked after while she was marching innocently through the mean wilderness."

There was a startling savageness in his voice when he answered her. "Damn it, Beth, do you think I was just going to walk off and leave you out there all on your own? I'd have gone crazy worrying about you if someone hadn't been around in case you needed help. You can call that chauvinism if you like, but I'm not apologizing for it."

Chauvinism? Yes, maybe it was, but Beth suddenly didn't care. All she could hear was the deep and unmistakable possessiveness in his voice, and all she could feel was this rush of joy. Then there was still a chance for them! No, wait. There was so much yet that didn't make sense.

She leaned toward him, anxious for his explanation. "But why? Why did it matter so much that I was protected?"

He didn't intend to roar it, but in his frustration over her stubborn refusal to see and accept the obvious, it came out that way. "My God, why do you think? Because you're important to me!"

"So important," she persisted, meaning to wring it all out of him, "you insist I climb those last five miles to the top of that mountain out there."

He scowled at her, looking impatient. "I thought I was siding with you against Charlie over the climb. Isn't that what you would have insisted on doing yourself, going to the end?"

"To satisfy the agreement, you mean?"

"No, not for that. For yourself. To prove you can do it."

He was right, of course. Whatever the arguments, she would never have agreed to end the hike here, not when she was this close to the finish. The ultimate moment of glory when she reached the summit would be her personal victory, and how could she deny herself the winning of it?

"That's right," he said, reading her. "And in case you've forgotten, I have a stake in this hike myself, and it doesn't have a thing to do with Hobart. That's why I mean to be right there with you sharing the finish."

What was he saying? Was he actually disclosing his pride and belief in her? Even more than that?

He smiled at her, but it was a bleak smile as he watched her tip her head to one side, her look both eager and worried. "The skeptical little Yankee wren is still with us, isn't she?" he observed.

"She has to be. Oh, Brian, why wouldn't I be nothing but confused and uncertain when you showed up in the office up there looking so brittle and uncaring. I didn't know you anymore."

"Is that what I seemed like?" he asked in slow wonder. "I thought what I was doing was keeping my emotions in check. And with a colossal effort, I might add. Because if I had let my feelings go, I would have wound up agreeing with Charlie and would have refused to let you risk the climb. But knowing what it meant to you—"

He broke off to stare at her, watching her struggle to sort out her turmoil. Back in the office he hadn't been able to afford to look at her, not without going all to pieces in front of Charlie. Instead, he had exercised that massive self-control, while longing to get her alone down here. But now he could drink his fill of her—the spirited brown eyes with those warm amber lights tugging at his insides, the chestnut hair that he wanted to free from the braid so he could comb his fingers through its heaviness down to her fragrant scalp, the swell of her breasts that even under a sweatshirt were so enticing to him he couldn't imagine how he had endured being apart from her all these long, miserable weeks.

"This is no good," he growled, unable to stand further restraint. "Me here, you over there. Beth, let me sit next to you. I can't show you what I'm feeling with this space between us."

"Brian, I'm not sure we—"

"Well, I am." He closed the separation between them with one swift movement. Dropping beside her on the sofa, his arms wrapped around her fiercely, saying more plainly than words, you're mine, and now I've got you just where you belong, and this time you don't get away.

But she didn't want to get away! Not ever!

He was squeezing her so tightly that she felt as if her bones were being pulverized, but she understood his intense, proprietary embrace. It was born of the same seething desperation as the bruising kiss that followed it, a wild need to prove to her how much she mattered to him. His mouth captured hers, lips branding her as his own. The wind went out of her as he deepened the kiss, but she welcomed his invading tongue, telling him with her eager responses that she accepted and shared his rough desire.

His hunger once expressed in that first violent onslaught, Brian seemed to realize that his passion, bordering on a rage, must be hurting her. The depth of his emotions shocked him. Immediately, he gentled his kiss, making it a mellow business of softly stroking tongue and hands that caressed instead of clenched.

"Now." He gasped, finally releasing her. "Now have I convinced you of what you mean to me?"

"Yes." She sighed, and then added recklessly, "I'm in love with you, Brian McArdle." What difference did it make which one of them said it first? "But you know that, don't you?"

He shut his eyes, and she could swear that he was actually saying a silent prayer of thanks. She had trouble swallowing the lump in her throat. He opened his eyes and nodded solemnly. She needed no words from him. His actions were enough.

"Tell me something," she said, her hand curling in his. "How could we misunderstand each other so much and so often?"

He thought about it for a second before he answered her. "I guess we were both afraid, Beth, and when you're unsure of yourself like that, you don't communicate."

She was amazed. "You? Afraid?"

"Yes."

"Of what?"

He hesitated, and she sensed that he was still holding back something vital. And then he told her carefully, slowly, "To commit to the woman I fell in love with on the Appalachian Trail."

"But why?"

"Because I didn't want to feel that way about any woman." His fingers, locked with hers, tightened. "Listen, Beth, you have to know this about me. I got credited somehow with this reputation for going through women like a reaper through grain. Well, it just isn't true. There were a few women, sure, and a couple I even cared about, but I wouldn't let any of them really matter."

"You were scared," she said.

"I was scared." He nodded. "Scared to get that close, because no matter what it looks like, Beth, I'm a traditional man, and to me getting close means marriage."

"But you were married before."

"That's right, and whenever the subject came up with us about my marriage, I acted like it really hadn't counted for anything. Well, I was lying. See, it wasn't losing Trudy herself that mattered. What we had was already gone, probably because it just wasn't strong enough to begin with. There were too many differences between us, like my wanting kids and her not wanting them, stuff like that."

"Then—"

"It was the divorce itself," he explained. "It was pretty rough on me. *Very* rough. I mean, I really hate the idea of divorce. I always have, and I don't care what the attitudes are these days. I don't know. Maybe it has to do with my parents' breakup. Anyway, the risk of marrying again . . . I just didn't think I ever wanted to or could face it." Brian smiled at her, a vulnerable smile that brought the lump back to her throat. "And then you sneaked up on me. When I realized how serious I suddenly was about you, how much I loved you, well, I bolted. I walked out on you in Harpers Ferry knowing I had to work this fear out of my system or give you up."

"And have you?" she asked him anxiously. "Worked it out?"

He grinned at her. "I must have. Because all I could do while we were apart was need you and think that it didn't matter how it ended for Hobart as long as I didn't lose you. I was no good without you, Beth, and after too many painful weeks of finally getting that through my thick head, any fears about marriage just didn't count. I only wanted to do one thing then, to rush up here and convince you that you needed a husband."

The lump was swelling in her throat as Beth realized how totally sensitive this man was, possessing frailties that balanced his strengths, qualities that only made her love him more deeply.

"So, do you?" he asked. "Need a husband?"

It might not have been the most original proposal, but she was convinced it would set a record for earnestness. "I think I do," she told him, freeing her hand from his to slide her arms around his waist.

He drew her close, his cheek riding against hers. "When?" he demanded.

"Mmm, soon," she answered indefinitely.

He bent his head, kissing the side of her throat. "That's too far away," he said impatiently.

His hair was tickling her nose. She wished he hadn't had it cut close at the temples, that it was still curling over the edges of his ears as it had out on the trail and that she could tease those crisp tendrils with her fingers. "You forget I have a job waiting for me back in Wisconsin," she reminded him. "I'd have to do something about that."

It was difficult being practical with his lips now working their way from her throat to the lobe of her ear. "Leave it," he ordered. "You can have a job with Hobart. You can advise the company on how to best protect the lands they develop, starting with the Sweetwater project."

"Brian, it's not that easy. There are things to be settled, arrangements to be made before we can be mar— Brian!" His lips were moving implacably toward her mouth. How was she supposed to fight that? "Brian, be sensible!"

"I don't want to be sensible," he growled. "I thought I was being sensible when I left you at the inn in Harpers Ferry so you could get on with the hike without any more emotional interference."

Beth hadn't the heart to tell him how much easier the hike would have been if he *had* interfered.

"And I thought I was being sensible when I agonized over my fears all those weeks while the only real fear that counted was that maybe you'd stopped caring. And you know what? It was a hell of a waste of time, all of it. I don't want to waste any more time, Beth."

"Brian, wait! Hang on a minute!" She tried to laugh him away. "There are things to think about. There's my apartment back home and all my stuff there and—"

"I have a house in Atlanta. A very good house. But if you don't like it, we'll build another house. And if you don't like the idea of working for Hobart, we'll find you a job that you do like."

Yes, he wanted her in his home, in his bed. He wanted to wake up beside her each day, to make love to her on long, lazy mornings. That was what he wanted, and he intended to have it. His wife.

"No more arguments," he insisted, mouth ready to claim hers.

"No more arguments," she relented.

He kissed her then, a thorough kiss that left her wondering exactly what arguments she had raised. She couldn't think of one. But Brian, lifting his mouth from hers, his raised thumb gently, sensuously tracing the contours of the lips he had just clung to so hungrily, was dissatisfied.

It wasn't enough. He wanted more. He wanted to gratify this sudden, wild longing to make her pregnant. He wanted to experience his child growing inside her. His wife, his baby.

Beth understood the clear challenge in his smoldering gaze, and she responded with a slow nod of agreement.

Both hands clasped around hers, he raised her from the sofa and began to back away toward the rear of the vehicle, drawing her with him.

"Here and now?" she asked as they moved from seating area through dinette.

"Here and now," he said, eyes darkening with a heavy, thick desire.

They were passing the completely equipped kitchen. "And what if your brother wanders in?"

"He won't. As long as there's one reporter on the premises, Charlie will be occupied."

They had reached a hallway, full bath on one side, wardrobes on the other. "But what if the fog clears, and they come looking for us?"

"Look," he told her grimly, still backing with her toward the master bedroom. "Do you know what I was like all those weeks we were apart? I couldn't concentrate on my work, I slammed around, irritable with myself and snapping at everyone. I was just plain ugly. Now, do you want to be responsible for more of that?''

''I guess not.''

''No, of course not.''

They reached the handsomely paneled bedroom. Brian released her to lower the shades on the windows, darkening the room to a silky twilight. Facing each other, they began to undress. It was like discovering each other all over again. She admired the strong, hair-darkened physique emerging from his sweater and jeans. He was excited by the lush, female body revealed under her sweatshirt and hiking shorts.

Naked, they came together on the wide bed, gazing at each other in a long, silent reverence. He began to touch her then, relearning the textures of her creamy flesh, wanting to make her his in every way. His slow fingers traveled from her bewitching breasts to her smoothly rounded hips and on to her soft, inviting thighs. He liked it when she shuddered over his explorations. It made him happy to give her pleasure.

He decided his mouth could please her better than his hands. Head lowered to her breast, he drew a rigid nipple deep into the warm moistness of his mouth. She began to writhe slowly against his steadying hands as his tongue swirled over one crest, then moved on to satisfy the other.

Brian fully intended to prolong the prelude to their joining, to extend the ritual with a series of lingering kisses and long caresses, but nature denied the plan. They had been too long apart, and treacherous memories of how exquisite the ultimate could be for them triggered arousals that demanded immediate fulfillment.

Inflamed, they fell back on the bed, Beth's hands and pleading whimpers urging him not to delay their oneness.

He complied, positioning himself between her thighs, his hardness seeking and winning her softness.

A wildness consumed them—a joyous fire of plunging hips, of Brian's face lost in profound rapture above hers, of whispered endearments, of a striving to answer not just an individual need but the needs of both.

Together they searched for the pinnacle, and together they found it, releasing themselves into the sweet void.

Afterward, when Brian had tucked himself against her side, arms wrapped around her securely, Beth lay there and basked in the miracle of his love.

Maybe the heavens, too, were celebrating their newfound unity, she thought a moment later as she noticed a distinct lightening of the sky through the translucent shade at the window. Easing out of Brian's arms, she lifted herself to her knees on the bed and raised the shade.

Sure enough, the fog was fast breaking up. Only patches of it now. She could already see the sun shining on the tip of Mount Katahdin above the treetops. Very soon, she realized happily, she would be up there conquering the last of the Appalachian Trail. But that wasn't so important anymore. What really mattered was that Brian would be close beside her, exactly where he belonged. They would go on up the mountain just as they would go on in life. Together.

"Hey, what are you doing? Come back here."

Beth turned her head to find Brian patting the empty place beside him. "I thought you were dozing," she said.

"No, I just had my eyes closed. Well," he admitted, "maybe I did drift off for a few seconds."

She settled back contentedly against his reassuring solidness. "I was checking the weather," she reported. "The fog is clearing off. We should be able to make the climb after lunch."

He grunted, managing to curl an arm under her and around her waist, as if he were taking no chance of her getting away again. "That isn't what's on my mind. It's the afterward I'm wondering about."

"Oh?"

"Sure. Just how we're going to get ourselves married. That's what I'm thinking about."

"Mmmm." Her fingers traced aimless patterns through the hair on his chest while she pondered the problem. "So," she suggested solemnly. "How about managing it on a turnaround hike? You know, Maine to Georgia this time."

Brian nodded with equal tongue-in-cheek soberness. "I'm agreeable, providing there are frequent stopovers."

"Oh, yes? Like for what?"

"We'll need one to get a license."

"That's true." She went on stirring her finger through his hair. "And one to buy wedding bands. Do you object to wearing a wedding band?"

"No, I want to."

"That's good. And, of course, we'll need another stop to find a judge or a preacher."

"And, naturally, after that," he promised in a husky, sexy drawl, "a long, long one to..."

* * * * *

SILHOUETTE® *Desire*™

COMING NEXT MONTH

#577 CANDLELIGHT FOR TWO—Annette Broadrick
Steve Donovan was the last person Jessica Sheldon wanted to accompany
her to Australia. Can two people who've made fighting into an art find
forever in each other's arms?

#578 NOT EASY—Lass Small
Detective Winslow Homer thought finding Penelope Rutherford's missing
camera would be a snap. But it wasn't so easy—and neither was getting
Penelope to admit that she found him irresistible!

#579 ECHOES FROM THE HEART—Kelly Jamison
Brenna McShane had never forgotten her very sexy—and very
unreliable—ex-husband. Then Luke McShane returned, bringing
home all the remembered pain . . . and all the remembered passion of
their young love.

#580 YANKEE LOVER—Beverly Barton
Historian Laurel Drew was writing her ancestor's biography when
unrefined John Mason showed up with a different story. Soon sparks were
flying between this Southern belle and her Yankee lover.

#581 BETWEEN FRIENDS—Candace Spencer
When reasonable Logan Fletcher proposed marriage to his best friend,
Catherine Parrish, it wasn't for love. Could he ever understand
Catherine's utterly romantic reasons for accepting?

#582 HOTSHOT—Kathleen Korbel
July's *Man of the Month*, photojournalist Devon Kane liked to be where
the action was. But with his latest subject—reclusive Libby Matthews—
Devon found the greatest adventure was love!

AVAILABLE NOW:

#571 SLOW BURN
Mary Lynn Baxter

#572 LOOK BEYOND THE DREAM
Noelle Berry McCue

#573 TEMPORARY HONEYMOON
Katherine Granger

#574 HOT ON HER TRAIL
Jean Barrett

#575 SMILES
Cathie Linz

#576 SHOWDOWN
Nancy Martin

Take 4 bestselling love stories FREE

Plus get a FREE surprise gift!